critical acclaim for
kate braverman's previous works

"Ms. Braverman possesses a magical, incantatory voice and the ability to loft ordinary lives into the heightened world of myth, and in using these gifts . . . she has succeeded in creating a work of hallucinatory, poetic power."
— *The New York Times*

"That Braverman is gifted, even prodigiously so, there is no doubt . . . her fiction is distinguished by the purity of language and boldness of imagery that seem to be the private stock of poets." — *Los Angeles Times*

"Jumpy, kinetic, and finally very powerful, a deeply felt piece of work by a very gifted young writer."
— Joan Didion

"Beautiful and poetic. . . . The captivating rhythm of Braverman's writing is hard to resist." — *Newsday*

"Unforgettable. . . . In a bravura performance, Braverman writes of women who drink, drug, and finally turn to A. A. — and she makes their stories grippingly fresh and insistent." — *Kirkus*

books by the author

kate braverman
small craft warnings

S T O R I E S

UNIVERSITY OF NEVADA PRESS ▲▲ RENO & LAS VEGAS

Western Literature Series

University of Nevada Press, Reno, Nevada 89557 USA

www.unpress.nevada.edu

Copyright © 1992, 1993, 1994, 1995, 1997, 1998 by
Kate Braverman

Manufactured in the United States of America

Design by Carrie Nelson House

Library of Congress Cataloging-in-Publication Data

Braverman, Kate.

Small craft warnings : stories / Kate Braverman.

p.cm. — (Western literature series)

ISBN 978-0-87417-321-5 (alk. Paper)

1. California, Southern—Social life and customs—
Fiction. 2. Women—California, Southern—Fiction.
I. title. II. Series.

PS3552.R3555S63 1998   98-12952

813'.54—dc21   CIP

The paper used in this book meets the requirements
of American National Standard for Information Sciences—Permanence of Paper for Printed Library
Materials, ANSI Z39.48-1984. Binding materials
were selected for strength and durability.

The author gratefully acknowledges the original
publishers of some of the stories in this collection:
"Small Craft Warnings," *American Short Fiction*
(Spring 1995); "Hour of the Fathers," *American Voice*
(1997); "They Take a Photograph of You When You
First Get Here," *Boulevard* (Spring 1998); "Pagan
Night," *Zyzzyva* (Summer 1994); "A Conjunction of
Dragon Ladies," *Antaeus* (Autumn 1992);
"Something About the Nature of Midnight,"
Kenyon Review (1993); "Histories of the
Undead," *Paris Review* (Spring 1994); "Guerrilla
Noon," *Southwest Review* (Summer 1993); "The
Woman After Rain," *American Voice* (1992); "Our
Lady of the 43 Sorrows," *Buzz* (1992).

This book has been reproduced as a digital reprint.

For Millicent Braverman

1927–1997

Mother, Grandmother, and Book Lover

contents

small craft warnings

small craft warnings

It was the winter my grandmother Danielle discovered candles and scents. It was her season of fragrances and textures, she often said that. If I had been younger, I might have thought she had become a witch, that's how intensely she breathed the creamy flames into her body, how her whole torso contrived to sculpt itself around the squat glass vases that held the fragrant wax in a kind of embrace.

But my grandmother Danielle was not a witch. She was merely corrupt and sociopathic. That's how my mother described her. It was January. I know that, absolutely, because my mother had taken me to her mother's house on my birthday and then left me there. I wasn't precisely abandoned. I knew my mother would return for me, that I wasn't in immediate danger. This time, my mother had gone to Paris.

She did this periodically, sold what we had managed to accumulate, took me to my grandmother Danielle's, and left me there while she went to Amsterdam, Rome, Vienna, London, and now France. She claimed it was research for her dissertation. She had grants and fellowships to attest to the importance of her scholarship. My grandmother and I both agreed, with perfect nonverbal communication, that my mother's European jaunts had nothing to do with furthering human understanding of sculpture or architecture, design or graphics or any of the other evolutions my mother's studies had taken across the decade.

"She can't find her own angle," Danielle told me, smoking a cigarette in the sun-room. Her voice was smooth with certainty and contempt. "She can't invent her own spin. That's why she spends her life staring at other people's faces and walls."

I didn't know what to say. There were evolutions everywhere. There were progressions, and the stakes inexorably rose. Now there was the complication of my grandmother's increasingly unsavory personal affairs. My mother had to arrange her European sojourns to coincide with periods when we were on speaking terms with Danielle. My grandmother was only in our lives sporadically, when she was between men. When my mother realized that Danielle was alone, she seized the moment, deposited me in the house on the hill, and stayed in Europe until her fellowship expired.

The entire process usually took five or six months. Then it was over. My mother returned as if she had only been gone for a weekend, and we resumed our life as it had been. I was used to sleeping on sofas and constantly changing schools. I thought it was simply another irritating and nonsensical part of childhood, like vaccinations and orthodontia, like the violin for a year, the piano for three years, and teachers who were blatantly unfair, who always favored the blonds who had doctors for fathers.

I was used to sudden departures and arrivals that disappointed, how nothing matched the description, not the apartment complex or the neighborhood, not the school or the park or the beach. Someone wrote glossy paragraphs in italics about deep-tufted grassy lawns, but that had nothing to do with my life.

"You'll learn plenty from your grandmother," my mother said, in a hurry. Suddenly, my grandmother had been revised, cleansed of sin and taint. There were always generous dispensations when my mother had a plane to catch. "Danielle's better than seventh grade. Trust me."

"What about school?" I asked. I wasn't even sure I cared if I went back to school again or not. The water fountain by the cafeteria was, in whatever school I went to, perpetually broken, the pretty girls with names like Lisa and Julie got better grades and school had already failed me.

I was leaning against a wall. Our suitcases were packed. My mother's were tagged for TWA Airlines. We both had sleeping bags. I hadn't washed my hair in two weeks. It occurred to me that I had nothing left to lose.

"School? School?" My mother repeated, lighting a French cigarette, staring at the rising gray calligraphy of the smoke and considering the strange syllable as if she had never encountered it before.

"Don't I have to go to school?" I repeated. I knew I was right. This was mandatory.

"Christ. You're so American," my mother decided, annoyed. "All over the world, kids have adventures. They hitchhike through Africa. They walk to India. Only Americans worry about school. They believe there's some correlation between civilization and education," she postulated, exhaling smoke.

"Is there?" I demanded.

"Of course not, you idiot," my mother yelled. "Look at this country." Then we drove to my grandmother's house.

My grandmother had a real house in the hills above Santa Monica. My mother and I always lived in apartments—in an interminable hell of graduate-school limbo—was my mother's description. "Dante couldn't have imagined this," my mother once said. She was talking about Van Nuys.

I was momentarily stunned when first seeing Danielle's house again, how substantial it was on the top of the hill, after the exactly one hundred and seven blue flagstone steps you had to climb to the front door. The door was behind a gray iron lattice. You had to be buzzed through the bars, which were twined with bougainvillea and wisteria. It was like a form of blue initiation.

"Do you know what style house this is?" my mother asked.

I considered colonial, traditional and contemporary, Cape Cod, California bungalow, English country, the classic Spanish of the late '20s. I looked at my mother's face, searching for clues. She was wearing her anonymous airport persona, no makeup, a scarf in her hair, blue jeans and layers that made her appear unattractively large. The look that said I'm not interesting on any level, don't mug or rape or bomb me. I was still sorting through possible architectural styles when my mother said, "It's called Marrying Well Repeatedly." She laughed.

Danielle's house was made from the sorts of materials my mother and I never had, wooden floors in fine vertical strips, enclosed orange tile patios that always felt cold under my feet, built-in cabinets and built-in book shelves in a dark wood that glistened as if it had just been polished. The house seemed not built or constructed but rather composed. Danielle had real canvas paintings on her walls, and whole sides of rooms were glass and looked down at the canyon and, farther, the city.

At night, I thought I was experiencing vertigo, watching the lights of Los Angeles that seemed to want to rise to meet the lights of the helicopters and planes that were landing. The light was everywhere alive, like an entity, and it seemed volitional, capable of choosing its own function, whether it wished to be a blue airport guide light or one lone green beacon floating on a buoy in the Santa Monica Harbor. Or a lemon-yellow porch light, a traffic light with three predictable phases or something more dazzling, like a display-case window strung with multiple bulbs flaunting their possibilities like a litter of gold and amber things I imagined sounded like bells. The city could be a kind of music if one was attentive and knew how to listen.

Then my mother was buzzing us through the iron lattice. I knew I was already learning to listen in an entirely new way. There were aviaries of color strung on invisible wires. There were transformations in sequences of sunlight and moonlight and smoke. There were chimes and chords inside stones and ways to open them, gut them, make them reveal their secrets of wind and rain. Then my grandmother opened the door.

I remember this particular visit as being not a night sojourn but rather an afternoon one. I think of my grandmother in her study with the door closed and half a dozen vanilla candles burning. She made rooms into rituals. She had housewarmer candles in heavy squat glass vases, and she would lean over them as they burned, breathing the vanilla smell deep into her body. I thought of exotic cargoes in the holds of ships, mangoes and Chinese vegetables in colors like glazed violet and cerulean. That's how she was taking the odor into her lungs, like she was a vessel containing it. I recognized bodies were for storage and transport.

"I never understood opulence," my grandmother said. It was during my first week back in her house. "I never understood taste or smell. I never had the ABC's."

She is elegant and sad, grave, her face like pewter. She is at her desk, her bare feet pressed into a flower-print Moroccan rug. A man who loved her or loved her money gave her that rug, and she would rub her feet into it. I wanted to peel off pieces of her skin and, like flower petals, keep them pressed between pages of books I would never lose.

In my memory of this visit, it is always winter in her study, the smallest room in the house. It is completely permeated with her fragrances. She is holding a glass-encased candle in her two hands, breathing the flamey vapor in, eyes closed. I think she could eat it, like a sacred food, a wafer, a bit of unleavened bread. I watch as she bends her face so close to the fire, her bangs are sometimes singed. I smell burned hair then, mixed in with the vanilla. It is like a sour red wire in the midst of what I imagine melted orchids smell like, something bewitched and lacquered. I thought magic was something that could be identified, cut out and laminated, like a photograph in a wallet.

"Vanilla shares the same properties as orchids," Danielle told me. "The Empress of China ate orchids. She smoked opium. The combination drove her mad."

My grandmother's voice was hoarse, rough edged, like she had opened her mouth to too much wind. It was a throat things had blown into, autumn leaves the red of maples in abrupt transit, leaves russet and auburn. And rocks, and the residues of olive and almond trees with their sweet and subtle scents.

"Do you hear her voice? That's what forty years of pot smoking will do for you," my mother had once said. "That woman must eat nails."

I thought there were mysterious essences, ways of being transmuted that came through the skin. I must have thought sex was like that, some conjunction of rain-forest night-blooming flower that entered you and changed you forever. I lacked systematic processes of discrimination then. I lurched between beacons of intuition, rage and sorrow. I knew what the stones know in their pretense of sleep. I knew city lights longed to be freed from their flagrant neon signs, from their overly representational prisons. They dreamed of being released, allowed to loiter instead in stained-glass cathedrals. They wanted to pour their bodies into the faces and capes of saints. I believed in immaculate conception and spontaneous combustion. I believed in aliens from outer space and vampires, prophecy and the resurrection of the dead. I had déjà vu many times each day. I was thirteen.

My grandmother was in her study, reading sporadically, underlining passages in yellow Magic Marker. She was saving sections of poems and novels for me to read later, even though she knew I probably wouldn't. I wasn't even going to junior high school anymore. But that was the least of it. Danielle said everything she loved would be out of fashion by the time I was an undergraduate. Pablo Neruda. Octavio Paz. T. S. Eliot. Sylvia Plath.

"I know," I told her, with mock sympathy. "There won't even be books when I grow up. The whole world will be on-line."

My grandmother shrugged. "Oh, that," she said, dismissing the future she had so recently lamented with a flick of her wrist. "That's irrelevant. I finally understand all gestures are egocentric. This has nothing to do with you," she said, holding the yellow pen in the vanilla-thickened air, as if she was leading an invisible yellow orchestra. I imagined she was conducting something composed entirely of brass, some real instruments, others that were creatures, alive, like rare insects with intricate wings that could be taught when to buzz and when to be mute.

I thought my grandmother could read minds. I thought she had mastered telepathy. There were burning candles all over the house and I thought she would die from fire or smoke inhalation before she died from heart disease. Heart disease sounded vague and open to interpretation, phases, and gradations. It lacked definite borders. It seemed like something creeping so slowly, one could forget about it entirely. It would never march far enough to catch my grandmother at the top of one hundred and seven perfect stone stairs a man who had loved her had built for her. It had taken him an entire summer, dawn to dusk. My grandmother with her permanently blond hair, with her size-six figure, with her tennis games and her convertible sports car. She was too fast for this disease. After all, my grandmother was the keeper of the scented flame.

I believed Danielle was somehow camouflaged by her fragrances and how they folded invisible leaves and fronds around her shoulders, her suddenly too thin neck. I thought nothing could find her beneath that woody vanilla, that startled, burned, sweet whiteness that wasn't magnolias or moonlight, not roses with tiny baby mouths, but something intrinsic to skin itself. That's what gave the vanilla its poignancy. It was the way it interacted with my grandmother's flesh, mysteriously, like a night forest where anything is possible.

I sensed there were confusions in her skin. There were always too many possibilities. Her body continually betrayed her, in one way or another. First there had been the men too young for her, long-haired men who took drugs and didn't have jobs. The men Danielle collected that forced my mother to repeatedly shun her. There were long periods when my grandmother was viewed as contaminated. We could not visit. She was living with a bass player from a second-rate San Francisco band.

"Not even San Francisco. They're from a garage in Vallejo. An opening act in its one best moment," my mother had assured me.

That was Danielle's most recent lapse, a liaison with a man thirty years younger than she. I had glimpsed them on the street once, purely by accident. He was blond like my grandmother and slight, thinner than she was. I had at first thought he was a woman. Then my mother said I could not visit, could not spend the night in the house on the hill where I had my own bedroom painted in my favorite shade of purple, August Lilac. This man was the worst yet, my mother informed me. The ultimate blond bimbo, she called him, and because he was now officially living in the house on the hill, I was not even allowed to telephone.

It took two years for the blond man to pass from my grandmother's house and life, and there were details my mother didn't even want to discuss. Something about the paintings and the car, something about tailored suits and the silver, something that had nothing to do with burglary. Now there was the matter of how my grandmother's body was again betraying her, this time with the heart disease.

It was the first year I was officially a teenager and I was

hungry for symbols. I thought I possessed an innate capacity for metaphor. My grandmother crossed borders with her skin and now her heart was rotting. My grandmother gave herself to bad men, men who were merely opening acts, salaried players, for Christ sake, my mother had said, and now, as a result, she was going to die.

My beliefs about death were ambiguous, barbaric, phobic. I closed my eyes and entered a realm of phantasmagoria. Sometimes I did not even need to close my eyes for this to occur. I believed rooms were haunted. I thought there were creatures caught between worlds, some warp in the space/time continuum that existed just behind my left shoulder. I entertained the notion that death was the consequence of bad thoughts and immoral actions. I was convinced that there were machines for reading thoughts and decoding images and if one strayed, graphically, sexually, a kind of plaque formed in your arteries. After enough such nights, you would need open-heart surgery, a bypass and a transplant and even that probably wouldn't work.

If Danielle needed it, I would give her my heart. I wanted to write a will, bequeathing my organs to her if I was shot or killed in a car crash. Then I realized my grandmother was too beautiful for death. Her skin was very white, it reminded me of her porcelain teacups, which she always drank from, the bone-thin cups with their gold rims and tiny violet flowers like a faint pulse on their sides. It was like they were breathing.

We often had tea together in the late afternoons. "Use objects," Danielle said, "or they're just boring pretensions." She was pouring tea from a pot that was three hundred years old. It had belonged to a warlord's fourteen-year-old concubine. My grandmother had carried it back from China herself.

I could watch her drink tea indefinitely, for afternoons or years. She had long blondish hair with a hint of red and freckles across her face and arms. Her eyes were huge and completely blue, so blue they looked painted. They were a blue I rarely saw in human beings. They reminded me of chemicals and bodies of water in certain seasons, fall perhaps, when the wind blows from the north. Danielle wore tight black lace leggings under miniskirts and very high heels, no matter where she was going. She looked nothing like me. I was much darker, olive skinned, and I was heavy, my bones were big, my head and feet and hands were larger than hers.

"You're sturdy," Danielle reassured me, smoking a cigarette I knew contained marijuana. I could smell it. "You'll live through the winter. What's wrong with that?"

It was the real, not metaphorical winter that I was thirteen and I wasn't going to school. Danielle never brought up the subject. After all, only Americans were compulsive about attending classes. The rest of the world spent their time having adventures, creating sculptures and paintings and enjoying good medical care. They went to palaces to live with warlords. As if reading my thoughts, Danielle said, "Let's do something exciting. I want to learn to sail."

She made two quick phone calls, and it was done. Everything seemed to be happening so fast. The space between ideas and their slow enactment was diminishing, and I was glad. We drove the red convertible Jaguar to the marina, and a man named Gordo appeared with a sailboat and a smile.

It was a California February rocked clean by storms, by fires and floods in the hills, by an earthquake, by elements that had scrubbed and anointed it. It was the clean-to-a-subatomic level that only California knows in the pause between disasters, in its intervals of pure color. These are the stalled moments when you know Los Angeles is chartreuse and lime. These are the subdued tropics where the green molts along the alleys and boulevards between the red of the poinsettias and the tanning of the sycamores. It is in February in Los Angeles that you know redemption is cyclic and eternal, indigenous like the palms and the desert winds and the crumbling cliffs above the Pacific.

Gordo motored us out of the marina. First, he put up the mainsail and then, as we left the artificial channel and entered the gray-blue bay, he raised the headsail. There were reasons for what he was doing; he was explaining the order of procedures to Danielle, the special knots the ropes required, how they must be rolled away, but I wasn't listening. The sails were called sheets, and Danielle said, "That's one thing I've always been good with."

"I can sure see that," Gordo answered with a laugh. He looked at my grandmother, but he couldn't see her withered heart, how the vessels were collapsing. Her cargo would be trapped. It would be lost at sea, mingling itself with doubloons and heirloom linen, with pianos and trinkets, with silver music boxes and love letters and all the things that never reach home. Danielle wasn't going to return to her port of origin, either.

We were sailing the harbor, which I decided was a kind of gray-hazel, capable of blue or green. It was a substance for a sorcerer. There were unknown variables. I could see the Santa Monica Mountains rising behind what looked like toy buildings. The mountains were the color of festering jade. It was suddenly very cold. Afternoon was like a slap, and I thought, yes, of course, it is in the air that we are redeemed.

I was standing next to Danielle. She leaned over to me suddenly and whispered in my ear, "What if one life isn't enough? What if three dimensions aren't right?" She was staring at the deceptive shifting bay, at the fluid mirror. "What if I can't find the coordinates home?"

"But you can," I said, without hesitation. It wasn't an act of kindness. It wasn't deliberate or contrived. It was like breathing in and out. I loved her.

After that, we drove to the dock almost every day. I had begun to see the city with a new clarity. The boulevards were festooned with desiccated ornamental plum trees and leaves that looked like leather pouches. I thought I could live off the land if I had to. There were hybrid hibiscus near the fence by the dock. They were the size of a clenched fist or a stabbed heart. No one asked me about school.

Our teacher, Gordo, would be waiting with his down vest over a denim shirt, with his smell of cigarettes and cold bay. My grandmother would not remove her high heels until we were already on the sail boat. She seemed small in her tennis shoes, close to the ground and her coffin. We usually had the same boat, the *Gabrielle Rose*. The name was painted in pink cursive letters. But the stern didn't indicate where it was from. Los Angeles had somehow taken over the world. It went without saying.

Then we were motoring out to the bay. We were attaching the halyard to our mainsail. We were cleating our ropes. We were unfurling the headsail with our winch. We were working our sheets, setting our course, aiming north to Malibu or south past the airport. We were on a broad reach, a close haul. We were tacking to starboard, we were jibing to port. The ocean was a hall of blue mirrors with a kinetic language. There were stairs down, currents and reasons.

The air was so utterly without interruption that it wasn't air as it is ordinarily known but rather an avenue for deciphering. There was no residue, no litter of foul pastels. Everything was abnormally etched the way white rock is. I could see the details on the individual houses and condominiums near the shore. I could identify their balconies, their sun decks, their garden roofs with banks of assertive red geraniums.

I would duck as the mainsail swung and my grandmother yelled, cheerfully, "Hard a-lee," into the agitated wind. I thought she was saying "heartily," and somehow talking about her heart, how it was dissolving in her chest cavity, how it was beating erratically, how it was somehow fading like stamps on an old passport. Where we enter and where we depart, all of it fading.

I thought of tattoos, how they too were blue and how

they faded. I considered the question of whether or not you could actually see a tattoo fade. This would only be possible if you were able to watch time pass. It would be a matter of adjusting the machinery. Watching time pass was a sort of paradox. I spent my afternoons on the hazel Santa Monica Bay, constructing conceptual contradictions about time and space.

The last afternoon we went sailing was on a red-flag day at the beginning of March. We passed the red flag by the Coast Guard station and I said, "Shouldn't we turn back?"

I had been with my grandmother for nearly three months. My mother hadn't sent a single postcard. My grandmother was meeting with her lawyer and drafting her will. I knew a red flag meant small craft warnings.

Gordo looked at Danielle and shrugged. "Just the tail end of a real small storm," he said. "I wouldn't lose sleep over it."

Danielle studied the triangular flag shaking in the wind. "I've always liked red," she said. "It's festive, like blood and brandy. Let's keep going."

We entered the bay, and the wind was suddenly tame. It was the wind that returned after serious punishment, subdued and normal. We were on the cusp between seasons. I wanted my grandmother to live until spring. It occurred to me that there is no imprecision on the cusp between seasons. The zones surrounding seasons have their own identities, their own assurances, languages and passwords. This day the edges were elegant under a grainy pewter half-light that reminded me of a new razor. The place between actual seasons is filled with tiny roses in transition. There are murders and amputations in the garden. There are choirs on the sandy floors beneath oceans.

That evening, my mother would be waiting back at the house on the hill. She would take me away with her. I would stand at a window of a new apartment, looking for the gutted stars in their coral burrows. I would see the moon, in multiple identities, hanging like clothes drying on a balcony or a flank on a meat hook. I would start school the next morning with a headache and a bad attitude.

I would come to know dusk and abhor it, the stainless steel gray in which I saw something like fine spiders encroaching toward the stars. The stars were far above the stucco, abstract in their fatal distance, anchored in their sullen silver. It was better than lying down and the affliction of dreams. Later still, I would spend what remained of my adolescence trying to reconstruct my last frayed season with my grandmother.

I remember once, driving home in the red Jaguar after one of our first sailing lessons, we passed a homeless woman lying on her side on a strip of green in the middle of a boulevard. "That's courage," Danielle said.

"That's mental illness," I replied.

"You're so conventional," Danielle laughed. There was nothing mean in her tone. "Can't you imagine choosing vagrancy? No address or chest x-rays? No florist or priest? Only a vast clarity at the juncture. Do you understand?"

"No," I said.

"I wish I had her conviction," Danielle told me. We were driving east along Wilshire Boulevard, and I knew she was talking about the homeless woman. "Some women divest themselves of sabbath. Sin becomes a kind of flame, a blue friend warm in your hand. Some women divest themselves of answers. Cause and effect, balancing the checkbook, rotating the linen. Jesus. I wish I'd gotten a tattoo."

"Of what?" I tried to imagine her porcelain skin with a green rose on the shoulder. Or a heart, perhaps, with a black guitar in the center.

"A blue crescent moon on my thigh. Done in jail ink. Something I couldn't be put in the family plot with." My grandmother smiled.

What I remember with the most clarity is that red flag

March day when we sailed Santa Monica Bay for the last time. I had stayed up all the previous night, alone in the sun-room with its three-sided windows, knowing I wouldn't be living there long. Danielle needed a cane now. She refused to use it, walked with it slowly from room to room, holding it, like a misshapen star lily. Her expression seemed astonished, that she would have this wooden implement, that any of this would be happening to her.

I saw a shooting star that March night. I thought the stars were burning down like red flowers, poinsettias or hibiscus. I knew I would spend the rest of my life standing alone at one window or another, considering the heavens. I would be solitude, distilled and refined. I would be alone beneath the coral reefs of constellations. I knew they were merely somber russet shells, uninhabited bodies of water abandoned as they slept. I thought this is why we often wake and feel wounded. There have been splinters of star as we slept and some of these red disks lodged in our flesh.

At my grandmother's house, I could tell time by the bells from St. Anthony's Cathedral. Danielle came and stood beside me at precisely five. She was wearing a red silk bathrobe she had gotten on a trip to Thailand. There were red dragons and red chrysanthemums embossed on the red silk. You had to see the designs with your fingers. They were meant to be traced by someone who loved you. Danielle had taken a young man with her on that cruise. I hadn't been allowed to see her for eight months. I knew. I counted and remembered. I had a calendar. I didn't hitchhike through Africa or marry soldiers, but I kept track of things. Now her hair looked too thin. Her eyes were streaked with red. She was smoking a cloisonné pipe.

"What is that?" I asked.

"Opium," my grandmother said. "It's very hard to get. Do you want some?"

I said no. But after a moment, in which I heard the five

bells die like five distant bullets, the residue of a drive-by shooting hitting someone else's infant, I inquired, voice soft, "Can I sit on your lap?"

"I thought you'd never ask," Danielle said. She sat on a sofa in the living room. I perched myself on her thighs. The bells from St. Anthony's had not quite faded, had contrived somehow to remain in the air. The bells were a sort of net, a kind of tattoo in the darkness, an embroidery that lingered. Everything was the color of stained silver.

"Ah, the somber hour of church bells plying their trade through the night. Time for remorse and abstinence. If you have the time," my grandmother said. Then she put her arms around me, pressed me hard against her wrapped-in-red-silk chest, and wept, loud and broken. I touched the dragons with my cheek. Then she howled.

In the morning, we sailed on the red-flagged, small craft warning harbor. "Hard a-lee!" Danielle cried, again and again.

I thought she was talking about her heart, how there were waves in it, channels, eddies, sandbars, places where you must post triangular warning signs. We are all like that, with our hearts littered from the residues of dredging and storms. It is always a season of small craft warnings. You sail into it, face first, as if you were canvas. You consider only the essence of red, the core, with its festive implications.

We sailed all day, through the day, sifting its hours and increments into navigational knots. We cleated it. We reinvented time and travel. The harbor was filled with spilled cargoes from sunken galleons. There were silver Peruvian flutes and fine linens. There were white jungle orchids and bolts of white lace for bridal dresses with patterns you could only recognize with your hands. There were fields of white poppies and strands of drowned pearls, and everything smelled of vanilla.

Danielle was yelling something into the wind as the mainsail swung, her voice hoarse and charged from a variety of self-inflicted sabotage. Certainly she was talking about her heart and how it belonged to the sea and the wind and the fluid elements, tattooed and unfading, the deceptive hazels and silvers in which we do not randomly drift. And of all that occurred to me then and later, this is the one truth of which I remain absolutely convinced.

hour of the fathers

It was late spring, just after my twelfth birthday, when I discovered I had a father. It had never occurred to me to wonder about the specific configuration of who or what he might be. I assumed there had been some complicated natural phenomenon, like a lightning storm or a strange disruption at sea when everything glows. It had the sense of prehistoric ritual. But there had been no residue. My mother and I were always untouched, without tarnish, in the uninterrupted pale green state of grace that was my childhood.

Then it was May, and suddenly I had a father who had one leg, a father who was Jewish, who had been in the war in Vietnam. A father with a name. Jay. A name and no job.

"He never has a job," my mother said. She seemed cheerful. "He's what we call the walking wounded. It's become his profession."

We were driving to the Greyhound bus station to have dinner with my father. He had come down from Seattle, where it was too cold. He had a three-hour layover. Then he was going to Houston. It was part of the loop he was taking back to Miami.

Suddenly the world was littered with cities where I had never expected them. I repeated their names, Seattle and Miami. They glistened in the warm air like individual orbs, miniature artificial worlds that could be strung like beads. I had heard about the Wandering Jew. Perhaps this was why my father was roaming between cities. Perhaps it was genetic. It might be in my blood, too.

I wanted to remember everything about the drive to the bus station. I wanted to impart the images directly into my cells and fibers, into the molecular level I imagined then as being a kind of web, a mesh, a sort of tiny aviary where small stark birds flew. I wanted to chart the precise way I felt in the manner a fever is noted by points and a red graph. I wanted to measure my father-hours the way a river is drawn in a blue curve. I wanted to know the actual dimensions, to make calculations. It must have been in a slow spreading season when I believed, absolutely, in the power of miles and pints and decimal points, the ruler and protractor. It was when I believed in straight A's.

It already seemed, by the spring of my twelfth birthday, that the definitive moments of my life had come when I wasn't looking, when I wasn't entirely prepared. My first period had been like that, even though I felt it coming, a sort of turning of an invisible coil inside that felt like wire. I had been carrying pads in my backpack for months, but the actual onset of the flow, the trickle of blood that slid down my thigh and farther, streaking my leg to my thick white gym sock, had been a complete surprise, a paralyzing startlement. I had stood on the schoolground pavement, feeling confused by the afternoon sun, noticing, through a series of odd blisters like pinpoints of white explosions, how square and flat the playground was, how it was entirely surrounded by a high fence. It was curious that I had not observed it this way before.

That had happened the previous winter, when I had promised to be alert and somehow hadn't. I had missed the winter streets, how they seemed unusually greened, darkened, mossy, somehow bloated and rotting. There was a sense of the streets as so many wet amputations, stumps where there had been boulevards. And I realized later this was the first intuition I had of my father preparing to enter my life.

"There are the walking wounded," my mother said, as she drove, "and there are those that crawl and drool. Be prepared."

We were pointed inland on a sequence of purple boulevards and I knew it was a definitive moment. It was coming up on the horizon. It would have a name in neon and a parking lot. This time it wouldn't fail me the way the other events of my life had, like becoming a woman. And before that, leaving the apartment on Nightingale Lane and moving to the house in Santa Monica, how I had somehow forgotten to take a picture of my bedroom, even though I had a camera and months to pack. I had somehow failed to turn around as we left the driveway, missed my chance to imprint the building and the way my bedroom windows faced directly into a patch of eucalyptus and orange trees, how the air was always stinging with citrus. There must be a way to take a picture of that, the textures that reside without structure in air.

I sensed that something would intercede on the day we moved. There would be an inexplicable circumstance, a sudden blizzard, a message delivered in person, some astral aberration. There would be a reason why it was obvious that we should not go. But at precisely 9:30 the moving truck came, just as my mother had ordained. And I realized there was a rule of trucks and clocks. This was a kind of mesh, too, a secret aviary, a silent mechanism that also ran the world. The truck I had willed not to come drove up to the curb, we got in our car, and I forgot to look back.

Now, as we drove to meet my father for dinner, I could see there was a greasy quality to the sunlight. It was nearly June, the month of the cold mornings that spoiled every summer. It was always like that, the haze that didn't burn off until four in the afternoon and by then it was too late to go swimming. There were years when I only wore my bathing suit once or twice. That was before my mother began to take me to Maui and Kauai.

We were driving inland and the haze turned thick and heavy. It hung on the leaves that weren't glistening, really, as much as they were coated and dazed. Jacaranda was blossoming everywhere, with its uniformly excessive purple. It was a color I thought I could apply the word *tawdry* to. It was one of my special summer-project extra-credit words. And I realized that I had never really observed jacaranda before. The afternoon was thick with a vague fragrance I decided might be the way dog urine is in the tropics. It was an odor of decay and lamplight, of something getting tarnished on the inside where soap won't remove it.

I explained this to my mother, my sense of the afternoon rotting, and she laughed. "It's definitely spoiled," she agreed. "Ruined, all right. Bad to the bone. Jay will love it."

The jacaranda was incredibly beautiful, especially when it spilled into the gutters like a kind of purple river, hardly moving, lazy and stalled. It seemed to be strangling on itself. I wondered if I had invented a paradox, how something could be exquisite and simultaneously torn and suffocating.

And it was slippery. It stained the cars, everyone complained, even Moe. He was eighty-three years old, and every May and June he stood on the sidewalk, sweeping petals, muttering. But I had forgotten to turn back that day on Nightingale Lane, and I knew even then, without asking my mother, that I would never see Moe again. He was too old, and Nightingale Lane was too far away. It was across the entire city, which was a sort of aviary of boulevards and cement, and I could never walk that far. My mother wasn't going back. My mother hated nostalgia, photographs from vacations, souvenirs of where we had once been. She called it Americana and said it made her nauseous. And the jacaranda stained feet and carpets. I had learned to wear sandals on sidewalks where the petals had fallen. I had several times slipped and skinned my knees.

It is odd, but I believe this was the last day I saw jacaranda for the rest of my childhood. I did not see it again until I was an adult, and it abruptly reappeared. My mother and I were walking across the parking lot, into the moment that was father, which opened like a soft wound. Spring vanished and the landscape was gone, and in their place was my father, Jay.

My mother introduced us, awkwardly. I reached out to shake hands and he stared at my arm. Everything was stalled and off balance. My father was wearing black sunglasses, a navy-blue coat that looked both wet and dusty, and he didn't smile. He was smoking a cigarette. We finally shook hands, and I understood why certain gestures are called wooden. My father, Jay, walked with a limp and a cane. His cane was fantastic, a reddish wood he said was mahogany. It had a silver band at the bottom and a snake that coiled, silver, along the side. The head of the snake formed the handle. Its mouth was open; a silver tongue protruded from it.

"I don't take that VA crap," my father said, following my gaze, explaining his cane. "That aluminum shit. What you see here is handcarved. This is a nine hundred dollar job."

I didn't know what to say. Everyone kept looking at their watches and the clock on the wall of the restaurant where my mother and I ordered salads. My father ordered soup and a well-done steak, and he ate everything on his plate including the garnish, which he called the best part. My mother went to pay the check.

"Did you really kill people?" I asked.

"Where?" My father looked around the restaurant.

"In Vietnam," I said.

My father lit a cigarette. His eyes were half-closed, as if something more than smoke were clawing at them. There were invisible wires strung in the air, camouflaged the color of dusk; a person could trip. "What you have to understand is this. It was very dark. There was lots of confusion. Everything happened so fast."

After that first appearance near my twelfth birthday, after that first furious passing, when we walked him across a parking lot to a bus that had the word *Dallas* printed in black block letters above the enormous windshield, my father would appear periodically. I thought he was like a comet with his erratic flash and dust. He would arrive in Los Angeles on the train or on a Greyhound bus. Sometimes he crossed the country in a sequence of trucks. He called this thumbing it. There were implications. His methods of transportation always seemed somehow obscene and hazardous.

"What does it mean to be Jewish?" I asked on that first ride home. This was something new and completely unexpected that I had become, like a woman who bled, like a woman with a one-legged father.

"I asked myself that once," my mother laughed. She had smoked a cigarette with Jay. Now she was smoking another. I had never seen her smoke before. "Standing in his mother's house. It was Malibu. On the ocean. A grand piano. A Miró. Minor, but I recognized it across the room. I took a deep breath. Imagine me, a girl from the projects. I couldn't breathe enough of that Jewish air."

"Then what?" I was also holding my breath.

"We got married. I got my degree. He enlisted, came back strung-out. A petty thief and part-time junky. You were born. They disinherited him. I filed for divorce. Then all the air went away." My mother shrugged. She had learned to breathe on her own.

My father, Jay, was a comet with a predictable orbit. You could plot his course. He existed in a sort of void, and we were a kind of gravity. I thought space was filled with the paths orbs made. I imagined them as a skater's blade marks left in ice. My father had a cutting arc. Space was cold and littered with the trails of what had passed, scars, indentures, lines like the mesh in aviaries. I thought of mathematics and music.

I began to understand that my father orbited around various race tracks across the country. He came to Southern California for the summer meet at Del Mar. Once he came for the winter meet at Santa Anita. But it is the summers in the rented apartments in San Diego that I most remember.

My mother made me visit him for long weekends. She often sent me with gift-wrapped packages on the bottom of Saks Fifth Avenue shopping bags with sandwiches on top. Sometimes she put the gift-wrapped objects—and I knew they were objects and not presents—inside my suitcase.

"I don't want to go," I would say.

"I know. He left his leg in Da Nang and now everybody pays. Even you," my mother said, lighting a cigarette, looking past me. Since that first evening at the bus station my mother had been smoking.

"You don't know how bad it is," I began.

I thought of the sounds I heard through the open windows of the apartments in San Diego. The fathers yelling at their daughters. Calling them tramps and pieces of trash. The way I tried to read on the sofa while my father got drunk and the people across the courtyard shouted at each other. In the nights in San Diego I felt physically assaulted, as if the air had been driven from my lungs. There had been a puncture, a slap or a kick. There was the sense of being violated and betrayed.

"Don't I?" My mother smiled. She looked at me. "He was six months away from graduation. The biggest firm in Laguna Beach wanted him. So he quit school and enlisted."

"Why?" I had never understood this.

"He said deferments were unfair to blacks and Mexicans who couldn't go to architectural school. Christ," my mother shook her head. "He called himself a man of conscience."

"Was he?" I asked. We were in her bedroom in the new house. It was early summer. Outside was a wash of mockingbirds and jasmine, the citrus of lemons, leaves being brushed by the sea breeze. I could taste the eucalyptus, pale, medicinal. The avocados hung like dark green stones, like triangular Christmas ornaments.

"A man of conscience?" My mother looked into the night. "Absolutely," she said. "Now it's time to pack."

Throughout high school, I made my visits to one interchangeable apartment in the suburbs of San Diego or another. I took the bus or more often the train, carrying packages wrapped in birthday paper that I knew were filled with lies, pretenses, or something worse. I could remember my separate journeys by the wrappings my mother covered the packages with. She usually wrapped them in birthday paper, little boys playing baseball on a glossy green field with matching red caps and uniforms. Sometimes there were balloons or pages of antique cars. There were the birthday-cake motifs with candles and hats and purple-and-gold confetti. There were floral prints with delicate white or lavender bows. Once, a large box with a soft rubbed away looking blue that offered *Congratulations on your new baby.*

"Christ. He's moving lids," my mother said once. "I can't believe it. He's down to moving lids."

I didn't ask her what these lids were. I knew they had nothing to do with jars. It was obvious they were meager and flawed and evil, whatever they were. The pretty wrapping was a masquerade. It was camouflage. There was something decaying and rotting inside, brittle and turning brown. It was something I wouldn't want to touch.

"I don't want to go," I was saying, watching my mother place several wrapped gifts in my suitcase. It was time for a floral print. I touched the tip of a pink peony. The packages felt like cold meatloaves.

"We owe him," my mother said. It was another summer. My mother had managed to quit smoking. It was a year when she wore a perfume that seemed tart and vaguely like ginger. She was writing advertisements for perfumes. She had just been promoted again. Now she had two secretaries.

"What do we owe him?" I demanded.

We owned our house. When he telephoned he called collect. He was in a phone booth in a rainstorm in Fresno or Portland or Austin. He had just pawned something. It was always a night that seemed to smell of vinegar and rusty metal and a wind with sulfur in it, old lightning, something hollowed out and burning quiet in the dark behind a packing plant and a trailer park.

Once when he came for the winter meet at Santa Anita, my mother dropped me off in front of the apartment he had rented in Hollywood. She gave me a bag for him that contained a new sweater, socks, underwear. She gave him a black cashmere scarf she had been saving for a special occasion. I wondered what we owed him.

"Karmically," my mother said. "He went to Nam so some Puerto Rican kid could stay home and OD. Now everybody has to pick up the slack."

I was sitting in the car with my mother. Hollywood was broken, shabby, even the trees gleamed rancid. It was a hot winter. The Santa Anas had been blowing. The air was charged. I was thinking of invisible cables, how if it got hot enough, the day could start buzzing, it could sound like a kind of song. I was thinking I would refuse to get out of the car.

"It's show time," my mother said. She seemed to be in a hurry. She found a Springsteen tape, pushed it into the cassette player.

"You know he only listens to music from bands that have at least one dead guy in them," I told her. "He says that makes it authentic."

"Authentic," my mother repeated. "That's a word you don't hear much about anymore. That man is a living museum."

"Listen. Are these visits with Dad going to continue

indefinitely?" I was angry. We were parked by the curb of a red brick building that said ROOMS on it in a chipped gray paint.

"No," my mother decided. "He doesn't have the attention span. He'll get bored after awhile."

"How long will that take?" Outside was Hollywood in a strange hot winter when everything seemed singed. The stray air over the gutted shell.

"He'll find somebody. A nurse at the VA maybe. That VA he likes in Georgia where they give him morphine." My mother glanced out the window. She was wearing sunglasses. A man with a snarling dog passed close to her window, and the dog turned and barked. She didn't flinch.

"Is that it?" I wanted to know.

"He might get busted. There's always the hope of incarceration." Her voice was completely indifferent. For the first time, I realized she didn't care.

"Do you think he might die?" I tried. I felt, suddenly, as if I might smile.

"He's suicidal. That's obvious." My mother looked at her watch. She pointed at the car door. "I just heard your cue," she said.

Then it was summer, and I would begin to feel sick on the train. California lay outside the window, as if it had stumbled and fallen down. Maybe it tripped a mine. A booby trap. It was convulsing under a thick greenish smog that called itself Irvine, Oceanside, and San Clemente. If I studied the air hard enough, I could see the architecture of individual strands of pollution. They were like so many sutures, fast stitches like the ones you get in makeshift hospitals near the front.

Then I was walking off the train. My father was leaning on his cane with the snake he claimed was sterling silver. I knew it was only plated. I could see where it was chipping and showing the bronze underneath. He was waving a white handkerchief at me like an emblem, a badge that admitted a wound. How could I possibly miss him, the one crippled man on the platform?

It was the Del Mar train station. It was near the ocean. And as I climbed down the steps, I knew what all condemned women know, what all refugees know. The game is lost. You walk down the steps, you enter the compound, one compound or another. There is barbed wire, real or symbolic, it doesn't matter. You know what the parameters are. It is simply a question of how much is going to be taken.

Then you are walking into the lost game. That's part of the ritual, how you enter of your own volition, how you don't run away. The man is sick. He spends part of each year in the VA, one VA or another. The man is missing a leg. He still gets infections, phantom pains. The man is dependent on a stick he pretends is encrusted with silver. He makes collect calls from gas stations on deserted night highways. He doesn't have a permanent mailing address. My mother gives him a credit card, just for emergencies, she says. This is a man who can't dance, climb a fence.

"He saw it as an existential moment," my mother said, her voice light. It was the night before I left for San Diego. "He made his statement."

I was sixteen. This would be my last summer. I was going to take a job next June, and after that I would go to the university. No one would ever again make me deliver fake wrapped presents to this man. He was my father by marginal technicality, a spasm and a shudder. As far as I could see, I didn't owe him the time of day.

"He's a downer," I complained. I was thinking of the train ride in the morning, how I knew California was ruined. It was limping along. It looked like it needed a cane. "He hates everybody."

"Not everybody. Just the old military-industrial-complex," my mother corrected.

It was a cool night. Blue jays and white star jasmine. The roses by the hedge. My mother had a new project at the advertising agency she now partially owned. She was vice-president in charge of creative work. She was designing a city. She had the scale model of the streets with mock cardboard houses on them, with grassy areas in green felt, with glued-on pine and palm trees. She was naming the streets, the entrance gates, the courtyard area by the swimming pool, the paths to the tennis courts. Marine Avenue. Dolphin Way. Canyon of the Coyotes. Driftwood Drive.

My mother put her pencil down. "He's terminally low-rent," she said. "But that's not a crime. You should learn to be cool."

My mother turned away. She was studying photographs of herself for the brochure that would describe the city by the ocean that did not yet have a name. She was looking at the photographs in an abstract way, as if they were the faces of strangers. Or perhaps they were people she had met once and briefly shared a train ride with, something had happened that she couldn't quite remember. My mother was holding a photograph of her face at a slight angle. It glistened as if it was covered with a kind of enamel paint containing preserving properties.

I wondered if my mother was cool, if it, too, was genetic. Something made me shiver. In the morning I was going to San Diego and she was going to Hawaii with somebody named Tony. She had already taken out her suitcase, made a pile of bathing suits and nightgowns.

Then I was walking off the train, and my father and I were riding a bus into San Diego. It was always a one-bedroom apartment that he rented. He let me have the bedroom while he slept on the sofa in the living room. The sofas were always a beige vinyl. The apartment smelled of him, of bourbon and cigars and what I had finally learned was marijuana. That's what was in the wrapped-with-ribbon birthday packages. My mother got him pounds of it, and he sold it in smaller units at the racetrack. He didn't have enough money to buy his own pounds. No one would give him credit.

"Even on his own diminished terms, he's a failure," my mother had observed. There was something flat in her tone that I did not quite understand.

I walked into the apartment and it smelled of some tangible despair, as if heartbreak could be opened like a sore. It was as if a certain emotional condition had an actual morphology, a size and a texture. There was a sour odor like a cold sweat that has only recently and partially dried, a sweat that comes from fear or a disorienting sickness, something like malaria. I thought it was a by-product of his psychiatric disturbance secreted through his pores. It was some eccentric biochemical poison that I could actually smell.

My father would remove his prosthetic device, push it under the table. He would hop and lean against walls, panting between lurches. His remaining leg was like a sausage. The skin was camellia pink. It looked glazed.

"History," my father drank his bourbon. "See my leg," he pointed at his stump. "My leg is history."

In the morning, we went to the racetrack at Del Mar. I found a bench in the shade. One summer visit I read *War and Peace* and *Madame Bovary* in one week. This time I had brought *The Brothers Karamazov* and *Crime and Punishment*. I chose books by their size. They were like bricks in the wall I built to protect myself.

My father was limping around Del Mar, making five dollar bets, selling quarter ounces. He would buy me the daily program. He asked if I had any hunches, if any of the names appealed to me, if I wanted to see the horses in the paddock, help him check for bandages. I said no.

"Your mother was like that. Sitting on the commons reading T. S. Eliot while they tear-gassed the town. I went to Nam and she got her degree on time. She didn't miss a beat. Not even one quarter late," he smiled. "Now she writes ads for hair spray. I'd never tell a lie that small. I wouldn't bother."

That night, it occurred to me that a kind of infection lay over these San Diego apartments. They were a sequence of Formica tabletops with views of fences embossed by singed red hibiscus and bitter oranges. There was a sense of flesh being severed and hospitals. It was there in the harsh overhead light bulbs, in the carpets that reeked of recent disinfectant and insecticide. It was as if transience was not simply a concept or a set of behaviors but an actual entity, and I could see it being preserved in a kind of formaldehyde.

"You college babes knock me out," my father said. He was drinking bourbon. He was smoking pot and cigarettes. "There's more history one morning at the track then you'll find in four years of college. This is the campus of life, baby."

It was an expectant air that seemed to demand something. My father sensed this. My father said the words. He trashed the night. He strung his own barbed wire wherever he went. He filled rooms with an aviary of sharp string.

We would eat a frozen dinner he microwaved. We ate it directly from the plastic container. Then the night came in with the sounds from other apartments. The fathers were calling their daughters whores, tramps, pigs. My father had taken off his artificial leg. His stump glistened red. We were playing poker using pills for chips. The yellow Percodan, the red Seconal, the blue Valium. We would ante with the codeine. They were white. I could hear the fathers in nearby bungalows yelling at their daughters, their Tracys and Darlenes, calling them sluts, calling them no good. I realized my father didn't hear this. It didn't register. It was beyond his perimeter. It didn't matter.

"I'll take you to Tijuana. That's being inside history, baby. That's where the books stop," my father said. "You could stay an extra day, maybe."

I didn't say anything. We were playing poker. His pills were the chips. They had different value. I studied my cards. I could hear the ice melting in his bourbon with the buzz of dying flies. I could see his cane with its chipped snake handle in the glare of the light that coated everything with a sort of plastic. It had nothing to do with illumination. The greasy light settled over my skin, stinging and numbing it. I thought of fossils trapped in amber and how the light was a sort of starch laminating this one particular moment.

I was considering the nature of this light as I boarded the train to Los Angeles in the morning. Soon I would be studying history at a college in New England in a city without a racetrack. As for next summer, I had a catalog of jobs for college students. There were listings for raft guides on the Arkansas River and dance instructors on cruise ships in the Caribbean. I could teach English in the South American jungle or in Japan or Korea. I could pass out blankets and vitamins in famine areas. I could clean up otters from oil spills. There were hundreds of possibilities and locations.

"I could ride up to L.A. with you," my father suddenly offered, quite unexpectedly. "It would give us a chance to talk."

"What would we talk about?" I asked.

I was boarding the train. I could spend the rest of my life boarding trains, following the tracks, the sutures in the earth, believing there was a destination, a depot of revelation. If you traveled far enough you could find the central mystery. I was going to leave this region that had so little to do with history as it had once been known. I was going to invent and map my own terrain, and this time I wouldn't miss a thing.

I realized that one could get trapped in moments, laminated by a certain lamplight, a sudden confluence of elements the color of brutally overripe lemons. It is always a summer evening strung with the accusation of slut and tramp sailing through the mesh of wide-open windows in rented bungalows in towns and cities near borders. It is always the hour of the fathers, when the mouth bruises and soils the night. There is the smell of rotting sun-sick camellias, bourbon and marijuana, shirts that should be washed. We are pinned there. Circumstances become dimensional and we are paralyzed, set in a sort of photograph we carry permanently like a kind of identification. When we are asked for our papers, this is what we are really reaching for. It is for this that we are frightened.

My father was on the platform. I could see him from my window so I looked away. The ocean was a slow, exhausted blue. I opened my book of summer jobs. I thought about rivers and mountains encrusted with columbine and larkspur, capitals with bridges and steeples and tiled domes. I could sense my father leaning on his cane, waving his white handkerchief that was like a flag of surrender below the decadent palms. I could have seen him this one last time if I had bothered to turn around.

they take a photograph of you when you first get here

They take a photograph of you when you first get here. They say study it. Take a good look. This is the before. Call it early sobriety.

I examine my photograph. I'm curled on my side on a cot. I don't have a clock. I don't know what month it is. I don't know what season it is. I don't know where I am. None of this bothers me.

I chain-smoke. I wear sunglasses at all times. I feel coated in a thick whitish film, like I've been painted with cornstarch or glue. I feel laminated. I feel like I'm stuck inside of a photograph of myself. I've been taped between pages of cellophane. I'm an inanimate object, a stylized representation, and I'm trying to break out. I've somehow coalesced in only two dimensions. I don't even know how or why I manage to keep breathing.

It's a stalled afternoon, and it feels permanent. The earth keeps spinning but the buildings don't fall. It's about gravity and axis and space. It's about inventing and memorizing hierarchies and pretending the debris matters. It's about some eighteen-year-old man walking through ice to his job selling shoes in downtown Boston. He walks because he doesn't have train fare. This has nothing to do with me.

A woman enters. Soft floral-print dress with more flowers stitched on the collar and cuffs. Pink sweater. Pastel shoes. Trying not to threaten. Fake pearl earrings. She's got gingham curtains in her kitchen. She believes in ruffles. She makes pancakes and waffles.

"I'm Susan. I interviewed you yesterday." Big smile. Blue eyes. I wonder how she'd look with a matching blue bruise on her cheek. Something the size of a robin's egg.

I examine my photograph. I am wearing a yellowish hospital pants suit. I'm barefoot and look like I smell rancid. And I wonder what Susan and I could have spoken about? Mozart and God? Women in Congress? The triumph of global capitalism as the millennial statement, its currency and philosophy? Or perhaps we talked about taxing crack and supplying addicts with clean needles?

This Susan exudes that Girl Scout troop leader enthusiasm that AA matrons get in their forties, instead of sex or power. "You're in Villa de Palma, Chemical Detox Unit," she explains. "You'll be here six weeks. Then you move to the halfway house."

I'm imagining Susan's face with a split lip. I'm considering the slope of her chin with a wired jaw. Could she still offer that mile-long, just-polished corridor of smile? I'm wondering how her face would look with one eye gouged out and an asymmetrical glass replacement. I decide to roll up in a small ball with the pillow on top of my head. I will, of course, never speak again.

I dream about Sapphire. Or perhaps it is not a dream but the reconstruction of events that only trapped images know. The photo in the album can dream at will. And the inmate in a locked ward. There are no comas, only invisible stairways into landscape. The maple in fall, burning red and yellow, loves you. Night is not a requirement.

Sapphire and I are running, crossing miniature square parks like gullies, grassy arroyos. We dart across boulevards, we jog down side streets. The dogs know us and keep back. The neon turns shy when we pass. The city is a body with crevices, places to nestle and curl. The Los Angeles night is like an ocean with currents and ports. I am a vessel and I don't need wind, don't need charts. Night is filled with the sounds of bells above waves, a seared harbor. It's always the eve of a fiesta, and there are too many sails.

"What is it?" Sapphire asks, sensing something. He listens to the darkness, tests the waters. He has his denim-blue notebook with his poems written in calligraphy in a special cobalt pen. He also has a flashlight and a semiautomatic Beretta with nine hydroshock hollow-point bullets. He's got a handful of syringes wrapped in a cotton bandanna.

"It's the laments of abandoned women. It's a night for mourning, for counting up the drownings," I tell him.

"You need a calculator for that," Sapphire laughs.

Moon glitters on his one gold earring. The urban night is intimate and specific. Sapphire knows darkness is dense with unusual currents. He's an alchemist. He mixes potions. He knows the proportions and how much powder and fluid are necessary to temporarily restrain evil. This is the impulse that made science begin.

We are winding down a narrow alley overgrown on the edges with bougainvillea and oleander. We are aiming west and we breathe easily. On balconies women water geraniums and dwarf roses, and I realize they have recently been betrayed or widowed. That's why they're howling.

We reach the pier, we know where the wire siding has been cut and we slide in. We have candles there, a mattress, blankets, silk sheets, a battery powered CD player and books. We have bags of cans we collected at the food bank. We have salmon and caviar and herring in white cream sauce. We have cherries in thick syrup and hearts of palm. This is what rich people give to food drives.

Sapphire offers me caviar. He extends a curled finger

encrusted with black eggs and I crawl to him and lick it off. If I bark, he will stroke my neck and call me good dog, good dog.

I am trying to frame a thought about harbors and wharves, how they all smell of ruined canvas and shells with the crusts of edible things dried, dead, like so many gutted black peaches. Nobody thinks about pearls anymore, or placing a shell to your ear. Everyone knows there are no answers.

Later Sapphire melts the tiny brown pebbles in a spoon. He fills the syringe. I offer my arm. This is how you make time and space stop. This is how they collide, lie down side by side and make love. It is the only conjunction that matters.

When the universe curves into itself it is a grave gesture, elegant with restraint and grief. It makes me think of thunderstorms and what I imagine Paris must be. There are boulevards where people stumble uncertain between lightning and premonitions. It is a festival of forgetting. It is a time of only cobalt and aqua and a burning rain. Rivers blister your hands. Well water makes you puke. There are no more lullabies, no more orchids, no more names for daughters.

"If we had a daughter, I would name her Ariel or Annabell," I say. "I could name her Amethyst."

"No way." Sapphire uses the bad dog, bad dog voice. It's a warning.

Farther up and down the beach are tiny fires from other night dwellers. They are cooking potatoes and heroin. I imagine history has always looked like this. An ocean where candles burn by corpses laid randomly on sand. It is a season of hallucination and drunkenness and too many reeds and guitars. Taverns are crowded with veiled women and convicts. It's a time of consecutive full moons. Orbs loiter in the skies. They seem superimposed, radioactive, multiplying. There is too much polluted silver. Its shine could make you blind. It is best to hide your face.

But you cannot look down, either. The tide drags in

strange sea mammals. They are bloated, the blue of fantastic rocks or flowers or stars. They wear the skin of waves. They are tattooed in the only manner that matters. This is what you cannot laser off. This is the sacrifice that lingers and defines you. This is the point of no return. This is how you know the world loves you.

"Do you love me?" I ask Jimmy Sapphire.

"Love is an inadequate coordinate," he says.

"Who am I?" I try, not certain whether I am thinking or talking. It is often raining inside my head. I am an oval filled with fluids. I am Prague and Lisbon. I have plazas and pigeons and bridges. Barges float heavy behind my eyes. They carry piles of silver haddock and sacks of mangoes. There are always bells.

"Who are you?" Sapphire repeats. "You're a gypsy and a time traveler, and I've given you a home."

"Is that significant?" I'm not sure I want this answer.

Sapphire considers the implications. It's a turquoise gully. It's a soft lavender gap. Everything about Sapphire is a form of blue. The bay he lives beside, the night he lives in, the way he distills fluid essences from powders and transports them into your blue veins. After this liquid pause in which ships sail and return, in this pale violet that could be a communion but isn't, he says, "No."

I listen to the waves. I think about stars and how Sapphire has a capacity for illicit alliances and what they may be worth. He has a gift for bargaining. He carries foreign coins that he claims are antiques smuggled from royal tombs. I have seen them, and they are ordinary bits of European change, disks of tin you'd give a bus driver in Amsterdam or Madrid.

He's a liar. His sequin shawls come from secondhand stores and thrift shops. They are not stolen tapestries. He can't read palms, either. He hasn't memorized the tarot. And he cannot predict death.

"It's not about truth," Sapphire would say. "DNA made truth obsolete."

"Then what's it about?" I would feel compelled to continue. I would be removing my sweat shirt. I would be offering him my swan arm. He can penetrate it with metal. He can saw it off.

"It's about amusement," Sapphire would say. "The dance of synapses. A few images. A metaphor between drownings. Admit it. You're never bored."

I have to concur. Nothing is dull anymore. My heart beats so fast I feel it's going to break through my chest. My organs are projectiles. I have learned certain things. I know the chant of fishermen. It is the secret of navigation and how to tame and seduce what swims. This is the litany that fills the nets. This is the method by which one masters the intricacies of breathing violet.

I have come to recognize that sounds combine in darkness, find other elements, transmute, become a fragrance, a pathway and a resolution. This is how one learns to trap stars and sculpt faces from clay. This is the sound rivers make and why women cover their heads and wear veils.

Sapphire has no comprehension of how much I've deciphered and remembered. In my dream, in my recreation of things as they almost were, in my subtle variations, I know I will soon confront him. This is inevitable. One twilight the color of crushed iris I will tell him he's a fraud. I will give him my evidence, assembled stem by stem, like a spring bouquet. My lines of revelation will be unassailable, the way calla lilies are, tulips and sweet william. I'm not a time traveler. I remember my address. I know where I live. But now there is only a sudden desire to sleep.

I toss and drift in forms of blue. I'm a swimmer, a virgin, a flame of water. I offer my arm.

"Beg me," Sapphire says.

"You are all things. You are why I pray. You are why I read poems and rob. You are a jewel. I place bouquets at your feet. I kiss your feet. I order schoolgirls to kneel before you. You will live forever," I say. I hold my arm out into the unsolid night.

"Convince me," Sapphire urges. He is staring into the bay. There are no lines, only gradations of violet. This is the color for penning love letters. It's a night for a tattoo.

"You are all kisses beneath palms. I wish you clairvoyant lovers who will promise you a calm world," I say. I will say anything. I am breathless. My arm is beginning to tremble.

"You're running out of stories," Sapphire says. He sounds resigned. He touches my arm with his index finger. "Let me tell you one. In Vietnam, the army medics inoculated village children. When they came back, they found a field of tiny amputated arms. They looked like doll arms. That's what the parents did. Sawed off the demon spots. Do you have marks of demonic visitation?"

I hold out my arm. My bruises are dark purple in the crushed iris night. They are tangled like grapevines. I say, "Yes."

"Do you think evil can be removed?" Sapphire is philosophical. Dawn is when he thinks he's lucid.

I say, "Yes."

Sapphire laughs. He keeps laughing. I am not worth answering, not with words or gestures. The water laps. The water beats. I shake and sweat and weep. I am lying on sand, but I feel underwater, like I'm drifting, partially submerged. There are equations of blue, there are geometries you can sail to and fluid architectures. They have their forces and properties. They have mouths but they refuse to speak.

In this place, they take your photograph when you first get here. I wear sunglasses when I sleep. They press into my face, sealing off my eyes. They were portals once, but I've cleverly soldered them shut. Everyone thinks I'm deformed now. But I'm camouflaged, preparing for secret actions.

This is how all discovery is made. First we see the interiors, what is most pure in objects, in a handful of wild oats, one white candle, the inexorable tide. Our voices are waves, and when we open our mouths to speak, the ocean flows in. These are not syllables or words but a sequence of broken amethyst. We learn to distill such waters and walk beside them, in a breeze composed of a subtle mesh, pale as a memory of larkspur. Then we hear foghorns and music from boats.

"You look better today," my counselor, Susan, says.

"How can you tell?" I decide to ask.

"You're not having convulsions," she replies. "You've stopped vomiting. And your color is better. You looked mottled last week, like marble."

Susan presents me with a paper bag containing a hairbrush, a toothbrush, and a bar of soap. I will not use these implements under any circumstances. Personal hygiene is irrelevant to a woman who doesn't know what year it is.

"Are you ready to tell me your name?" Susan asks, optimistically.

"Margarite," I say. I like the way it fills the air, like a woman donning a complicated antique opera dress, something with silk layers and rows of concealed buttons. It's a vivid name, a Matisse name, somehow tropical and magenta, but restrained. You could sweep down a corridor in such a name and there would be nothing improper about it.

"That's not true," Susan sighs, disappointed. She's an umpire for law and order. She keeps track while God is busy.

I have given her a different name every time she asks. Barbara. Maureen. Sylvia. Denise. Laura. Colleen. I glance at Susan, imagining her with a thick red scar running from below her left eye to her neck. Not a single scar line, like a knife makes, but rather something with branches like a river. The sort of scar a mountain lion or a jaguar might etch.

In a room nearby, someone is listening to Peruvian flute music. I heard it yesterday, too. I almost like it. I like what it isn't, namely Chopin and Mozart. Classical music makes me sick. My mother watched me practice my piano. She timed me. I would play badly, deliberately, thinking about rain and how my mother was pacing just behind my shoulder with a stopwatch. My mother never saw a house that contained a piano until she was twenty-six. That was the year she graduated from her first college. She attended the university in alternative years. In between, she was a grocery store checker. It took her eight years to get her undergraduate degree.

My mother always gave me music boxes, for my birthday, for Christmas, music boxes with porcelain ballerinas spinning on the carved or lacquered tops. I wasn't graceful. I wasn't even musical. What was her agenda, anyway? What was the subtext?

My father kept pushing Bach. I found Bach impossible, autumnal in all the wrong ways. It was beyond retro. It was like a wire mesh of rain, a sort of monsoon that could cut you. It was like a math class you did with your fingers. My father listened on the periphery while I thought about gray stones and bridges across pewter rivers where everyone carried umbrellas and believed Jesus Christ was the light at the end of the tunnel. It was worse than square dancing. It was worse than quilting.

"It's so unequivocally traditional," I used to try to tell them. "You were a revolutionary. Dad burned his draft card. Can't you see this is reactionary?"

"Don't be puerile," my mother would answer, wearing the stopwatch around her neck. "There are patterns to civilization. And this is one of them."

The Peruvian flute music, on the other hand, is cool. In this music, they have not yet invented the industrial revolution that leads to excessive punctuality or the failed experiment they call the nuclear family.This is the music of elements, untarnished, unrehearsed. It's clouds resting against mountains above cocoa leaves and one red flower surrendering to rain as if it had been born for just that seduction.

My father would listen to my piano practice while he was doing something else, thinking about the stochastic nature of the universe and the value of a disciplined mind. Whenever I think of my father, I want a hallucinogen. It's a sudden craving. I see paisley everywhere, and I want to melt into it.

I close my eyes, carefully, so they don't fall out of their sockets. It's possible I'm going deaf. It could be a side effect of the flute music. Or living under the pier for six months, with all the garbage washing up in the tide, old hospital gauze, soft unrecognizable objects that might be body parts.

I think about changing my clothes, but I'm convinced there's an aviary in my closet. There are acres of butterflies inside, so many, so thick, they could be a bolt of fabric or a silk kimono tacked to the wall.

I've always thought objects have a life force, personalities and intentions. I've seen wall hangings more interesting than the people who own them.

Apparently it's a visit-your-neighbor's-cell day. Some anorexic woman with a bad perm, really the remnants of a malevolent hair curling experience, has walked without knocking into my room. She seems to be evaluating it on a serious level, like a real estate agent, sizing it up, weighing the possibilities, how it would look if you knocked down a wall, put in a sunken alcove, bay windows, a balcony. You'd be shocked what a little hand-painted tile can do, a few oak shelves. I am still refusing all hygiene products. I am still wearing my sunglasses and hospital pajamas.

"I'm Bonnie," she offers.

"Okay," I say. "If that works for you."

"What's your name?"

"Debby," I reply. "I'm leaving today."

"Where are you from?" Bonnie asks.

"Cincinnati," I say. "My father was Iranian. He committed suicide. He died alone, like a dog, on the floor. He turned blue."

"That's terrible," Bonnie says.

"He molested me and my brothers. It was for the best."
I'm beginning to enjoy this visit. I bum a cigarette.

"Do you have any hobbies?" Bonnie wants to know.

"I collect rain in old jam jars, mostly," I tell her. "And
coins. I have a penny collection. I also bake breads."

She's only asked three questions, but if this visit goes to
twenty, I won't be able to endure it. I haven't asked her
anything and I don't plan to. She doesn't seem to notice.

"What are you in for?" Bonnie inquires. She's leaned
forward, vaguely conspiratorial.

"Please?" I read that phrase in an European novel and
I like it. Asking for clarification, but subtle.

"Drugs? Alcohol? Did you snuff somebody?" Bonnie
asks. That is question number five.

"Of course not. I'm happily married to an attorney. I
have two sons in Little League."

Bonnie smokes another cigarette. She studies the wall
as if planning to hang something cheery on it, maybe
some Monet haystacks or lilies.

"You're full of it," she decides. "Everybody knows
you're just a local junky. Everybody knows your pimp is
dead."

"That's a lie," I say, my voice rising. I don't believe her.
Sapphire is coming to spring me at any moment. I've
never doubted that.

"He's the one dead as a dog. Washed up in front of the
new Loew's Hotel. Belly up like a diseased seal. Something ate the edges. They had to identify him from his
dental records." Bonnie smiles. She's got buck teeth and
her hand is on the door. "Have a nice day," she says.

The person down the hall has switched to Gregorian
chants. It makes me think that at the edge of the world
there are walled courtyards where burlap-draped monks
kneel at dawn to open their throats to the sky.

I suddenly remember being in Golden Gate Park in San

Francisco with my mother. She was giving a lecture at Berkeley and we spent the afternoon in the gardens. It was late April and everything was blooming on cue. We walked through a recreation of a Biblical garden, each plant, flower, and herb something mentioned in the Old Testament. Then a garden where my mother bent down to smell each plant, the fragrant, the bitter, that which was like onion and lemon, and something like gin. My mother began to cry.

"I can feel the edge of my life," she said. "I've never felt that before. I was always moving. The vastness was incalculable. It was like the Pacific to someone in a canoe. I didn't think it had an end. But I have finally reached the border."

I looked up and saw the tops of trees, a domed building, something that might have been lilac or wisteria. My mother was talking about borders and I was looking for a guy with a machine gun in a guard tower.

"Now I know all city parks are the same. Hyde Park. The bluffs above Santa Monica. The Tuileries. Just paths beneath trees where people walk in varying states of heartbreak. Staggering between divorces and biopsies. And at the edge, one final row of lavender azaleas."

I couldn't think of anything to say. Her intensity was nauseating. It was like AA. There was nothing personal in it. It was late April. The wind seemed tinged with burlap and canvas and a sense of warm rain. When I looked at my mother, her lower lip was quivering.

"This is how you can see a heart as it breaks," my mother said, seemingly composed. "The eyes lie. And the voice. You can learn to control that. But watch the lips. That's where you can really chart it."

The Gregorian chant is playing still or again. It is essential that the song does not vary. It must sound as if ordained. It is the music you hear when lighting a candle, when you know it is a tiny captured sun you hold and the flame at the end is the first and last spark in the universe.

I do not believe Jimmy Sapphire is dead. I don't like the shape of my thoughts. I decide to think only in Spanish. It's a more fluid and fragrant language. The glare of the lamp is intrusive. I've been wanting to do this for days, pick it up and hurl it to the floor. The base is glass, and I walk back and forth through the shards. I don't feel a thing. Later I wrap my torn feet in a yellow pajama top I find folded in the closet, which is not filled with birds, not even a few stray sparrows. I look at the glass on the floor, the sudden splinters, the accidental precision of a randomly broken world, an anatomy you can actually grind your flesh into.

When my counselor points at my feet and asks what it means, I say, "It's a fashion statement."

It's apparently a day for group indoctrination. It's my turn to deal with the twelve-step do-gooders, the former pillheads and dopers who can't get the disease out of their system. It's a way of life for them. It's like golf. It gets them out of the house and gives them purpose. They say they're not a religious cult, but their whole program is about sin and redemption, God and prayer.

There are nineteen drug addicts of varying description in my group. We're supposed to be exploring our senses. Last week, while I was still locked up, they all ate oranges and talked about the taste and what it meant to them. Today, they're smelling perfumes. There are dozens of bottles and vials in the center of the table, and people pass them around like joints, taking a whiff or two and handing the bottle on.

Some gray-haired woman who looks like you think your grandmother should look before all the old women got face lifts and started playing tennis, is talking about what she calls female procedures and how she failed to learn them. She realized it occurred during her adolescence, but she had no friends then. Fragrance was something that came to her later in life, almost in middle age.

She never understood what suited her so she just purchased what was popular and expensive.

She holds up a bottle that contains the best-selling perfume of the year. She passes it around our circle and I
take a deep breath. It smells like a corrupted vanilla, a
genetically engineered vanilla, perhaps, laced with metallic properties. It is sharp, not like citrus, but rather like a
harbor that's been mined. The oil is thick and seems to
indicate what may be explosive properties. It's a vanilla
like an unexpected tattoo, a fire burn, or what happens to
a body when it's been two or three nights in ocean water.

There is nothing subtle about this scent. This is not a
fragrance distilled by tradition, one that asserts an ordered
world where you know the names of your sons before
they are born. This is insistent, almost strident, like the
core of instinct.

Of course, this has nothing to do with me. The old-
fashioned grandmother is saying women don't wear the
suggestion of lilac anymore because implication is no
longer enough. They demand neon scents now, mean
and inescapable, like a heat missile.

When it is my turn to speak, I say, "I have no thoughts
on this subject."

"I see," the leader, some big-shouldered man who
looks neutered, says.

"You don't see shit. You don't see a single thing. You
aren't even blind," I tell him. Then I limp out of the room.

They take a photograph on your first family-visit day.
They say you'll want to save it. They say it's indelible.

It's the end of July and all the blues have been used
up. They have been leached from the air. They have been
temporarily removed. They have faded. They are less
than bruises. My boyfriend who took the name of a jewel
as his alias doesn't come to see me. He overdosed and
something chewed off his leg from the thigh down as he
bobbed in the light blue early morning surf. Something
kissed his feet after all, kissed and swallowed in an act of

sublime love. It wasn't death but passion such as must be common on distant worlds, or in other times or regions. This knowledge is the fundamental basis of all rumor and nightmare.

My mother and father move slowly across the drying grass, through the day that has separated into frames in two dimensions. It occurs to me that they're moving slowly because they are weighted down by so much integrity it's hard to get any momentum going. My father, the draft-card burner and Bach fan. I've heard it all, the entire litany, how he was shunned by his petit-bourgeois family, left to fend for himself in Boston in winter. He was eighteen years old, without bus fare, hiking through ice to his job selling shoes, walking to six years of manual labor, roofing, plumbing, carrying boxes and bags on his back like a pack animal while all his friends went to med school. My father, almost dying twice in Massachusetts General Hospital from pneumonia.

We are all alone, the three of us, in a room with only one exit, and they are standing in front of it. It's a temporary lobby of some sort, with a piano, a bookcase, a Persian rug with mute flowers like petals floating in a bay. They look like severed mouths. They look like the last sound you make before you drown. No one asks me to play the piano

"I always knew this would happen," my mother begins. "I knew when you were twelve."

"Knew what?" I ask. I wear sunglasses. My feet are bandaged. The day is composed of sheared glass. Agate morning. Amber noon. Petty yellow everywhere. Stilted yellow. Stalled and soiled, urine and grease. I'm not going to play any more waltzes or sonatinas. I'm not going back to college.

"That you'd run off with some guy named for an insect or a reptile," my mother says. "Some lowlife called Spider or Scorpion or Snake."

I don't bother to correct her, to tell her I loved someone with the facets of a jewel. He exposed the underbelly, he unzipped it and I entered into the nuances and I learned how to navigate them.

"Don't you want to know how I feel?" I ask.

"We know how you feel," my mother says. "You were a bored college girl. Then a guy with a dirty mouth took off your dress. Now you think you possess the secret of the universe."

Someone from the staff arrives, a boy with a dark blue crescent moon tattooed on his right hand. He serves tea in porcelain cups with rosebuds and gold rims. I wonder how the cup would look with its golden lip bitten off. Then the boy takes the photograph. It's a Polaroid. I get to keep it after my parents leave.

I stand in my room while the sun goes down. I hold the photograph, looking intently into the edges, the periphery. I am trying to hear what they are thinking. My father is white in this black-and-white picture. His features seem dug in, as if with a scalpel. There is an absence of sound. He is not mentally calculating square roots while hammering a roof in Boston. He is not thinking about mathematics or Bach while walking through a snowdrift to a job that humiliates him. He has come to the end of equations, the final plaza where there are no bells, no cathedrals, no statues of poets, no view of the harbor. There is gray and gray only, and there will never be anything other than this moment when they carve a mouth for you with a razor. It is the concept of a mouth, an illusion, a sort of cartoon. It's a jagged hole and that's okay because it is the end of words.

I don't have to look at my mother's face. She has realized that at the end of her world is a row of lavender azaleas and one other structure she never noticed before. Beyond this hedge of indifferent vegetation, there is a room where they keep her only daughter locked.

There is a palm tree on the absolute periphery, outside the wrought iron grated balcony. There is a bench below on the lawn, and a paler area of shadow. I do not look at my mother's face. I don't have to. She is thinking she was wrong, with the stopwatch, with Chopin. There is no civilization. There are no patterns. There is nothing worth remembering, not orally, not with musical notation. You roof a house. You make a stand. Floating things eat your feet. Strangers violate your children. There is a scent of putrid vanilla rising from the plaza. It is mixed in with the blood and rags. It is the fragrance of some violent aftermath. It is a perfume for women who choose to live in a blackout, in a region where forgiveness has either been rendered obsolete or not yet invented. Prophecy. Superstition. The third planet from the sun is now and has always been a world of barbarians.

I know, from the feel of the photograph, from some essence in the fiber of the moist glossy paper, from some subtle interplay of light and shadow that travels through the neurons of my fingers, that my mother's lip is permanently quivering.

pagan night

Sometimes they called it Forest or Sky. Sometimes they called him River or Wind. Once, during a week of storms when she could not leave the van at all, not for seven consecutive days, they called him Gray. The baby with the floating name, and how she carries him and he keeps crying, has one rash after another, coughs, seems to shudder and choke. It is a baby of spasms, of a twisted face turning colors. You wouldn't want to put his picture on the baby-food jar. You wouldn't want to carry his picture in your wallet even if you had his photograph, and she doesn't.

Of course, Dalton never wanted this baby. Neither did she. The baby was just something that happened and there didn't seem to be the time to make it not happen. They were on tour, two months of one-nighters between San Diego and Seattle, and when it was over the band broke up. When it was over they got drunk and sold the keyboards and video cameras for heroin. Then they were in San Francisco and she still had the apartment. Later, they had Dalton's van.

Then they had to leave San Francisco. Something about the equipment, the amplifiers Dalton insisted were his, that they had accrued to him by a process of decision and sacrifice. Then they had to wind through California with her belly already showing and all they had left were their black leather jackets and the silver-and-turquoise jewelry they had somehow acquired in Gallup or Flagstaff. Dalton kept talking about the drummer's kit, which he claimed was actually his, and they sold it in Reno and lived on the top floor of an old hotel with a view of the mountains. They had room service for three weeks, and by then she had stopped throwing up. After that there was more of Nevada and the van broke again on the other side of the state. There was the slow entry into Idaho, after mountains and desert and Utah, and the snow had melted and then the baby they had almost forgotten about was born.

Dalton can't stand the baby crying. That's why she leaves the van, walks three miles into town along the river. When she has a dollar-fifty she buys an espresso in the café where the waitress has heard of her band.

Sunny stays away from the van as long as she can. Sometimes someone will offer her a ride to the park or the zoo or the shopping mall and she takes it. She's let her hair grow out, the purple and magenta streaks are nearly gone, seem an accident that could have happened to anyone, a mislabeled bottle, perhaps. Dalton says it's better to blend in. He's cut his hair, too, and wears a San Diego Padres baseball cap. He says it makes him feel closer to God.

Willow. Cottonwood. Creek. Eagle. She could call the baby Willow. But Dalton refuses to give it a name. He resists the gender, refers to the baby as it, not he. Just it, the creature that makes the noise. But it doesn't cost any money. She still feeds it from her body and the rashes come and go. It's because she doesn't have enough diapers. Sunny puts suntan lotion on the baby's sores, massage oil, whatever is left in her suitcase from the other life. Once she covered the baby's rash with layers of fluorescent orange lipstick, the last of her stage makeup.

Sunny has begun to realize that if she can't keep the baby quiet, Dalton will leave her. It won't always be summer here. There will come a season when she can't just walk all day, or sit in the mall or the lobby of the granite city hall, pretending to read a newspaper. She won't be able to spend the entire winter in the basement of the museum where they have built a replica of the town as it was in the beginning, with its penny-candy store and nickel barbershop and baths for a quarter. She won't be able to spend five or six months attempting to transport herself through time telepathically. She could work in the saloon, find an Indian to watch the baby. Later she could marry the sheriff.

Today, walking by the river, it occurred to Sunny that this landscape was different from any other she had known. It wasn't the punched-awake, intoxicated glow of the tropics, seductive and inflamed. It didn't tease you and make you want to die for it. That's what she thought of Hawaii. And it wasn't the rancid gleam like spoiled lemons that coated everything in a sort of bad-childhood waxy veneer flashback. That's what she thought of Los Angeles where they had lived for two years. In Los Angeles, afternoon smelled of ash and some enormous August you could not placate or forget. Los Angeles air reminded her of what happened to children in foster homes at dusk when they took their clothes off, things that were done in stucco added-on garages with ropes and pieces of metal and the freeway rushing in the background like a cheap sound track. It was in sync, but it had no meaning.

This Idaho was an entirely separate area of the spectrum. There was something unstable about it, as if it had risen from a core of some vast, failed incaution. It was the end of restlessness. It was what happened when you stopped looking over your shoulder. It was what happened when you dared to catch your breath, when you thought you were safe. Sunny feels there is some mean streak to this still raw, still frontier, place. This land knows it gets cold, winter stays too long, crops rot, you starve. This land knows about wind, how after storms the clouds continue to assemble every afternoon over the plain, gather and recombine and rain again and this can go on for weeks. Her shoes are always damp. Her feet are encased in white blisters. Always, the thunderheads are congregating and mating, and their spawn is a cold rain.

Some days the clouds are in remission, ringing the plain but staying low. On such afternoons, the three of them go down to the Snake River. They follow a dirt road to another dirt road, and they've been instructed where to turn, near the hit-by-lightning willow. They park on a rise above the channel. Dalton leaves his guitar in the van and padlocks it, walks ahead of her and the baby with the fishing pole over his shoulder. They walk beneath black branches, find the path of smooth rocks down to the bank leading to a railroad bridge. It's a trestle over the Snake made from railroad ties with gaps between them and the tracks running down the center. This is how they cross the Snake, reach the other bank where the fishing is supposed to be good. There are tiny grassy islands Dalton can roll up his black jeans and wade out to. Dalton traded somebody in town for a fly-fishing rod. He probably traded drugs for the rod, though she realizes she hasn't seen her black leather jacket for more than a week.

On Sundays yellow with orioles and tiger monarchs and a sun that turns the grasses soft, Dalton takes them fishing on the far bank of the river. One late afternoon he caught four trout. Sunny could see their rainbows when the sun struck their skin. They looked sewed with red sequins. They were supposed to be sixteen inches. That was the rule for the South Fork of the Snake. Their trout were smaller, seven and eight inches, but they kept them anyway, cooked them on a stick over a fire they made near the van. Dalton said the eyes were the best part and he gave her one and it was white as a pried-open moon and she ate it.

Now she is walking into a yellow that makes her feel both restless and invigorated. A yellow of simultaneity and symbols and some arcane celebration she can vaguely sense. When she ate the trout eye, it was like a crisp white stone. She thought of rituals, primitive people, the fundamental meaning of blood. If one mastered these elements, it might be possible to see better in the dark. She shakes her head as if to clear it, but nothing changes. Her entire life is a network of intuitions, the beginning of words, like *neon* and *dome, pine, topaz, shadow,* but then the baby starts crying.

Sunny knows it's all a matter of practice, even silence and erasure and absence. What isn't is also a matter of practice. In the same way that you can take piano or voice lessons and train yourself to recognize and exploit your range, you can also teach yourself not to speak, not to remember. That's why when Dalton asks what she's thinking, she says, "Nothing." It's a kind of discipline. What she's really thinking about is what will happen when summer is over. What will happen if she can't make the baby stop crying?

Sometimes when she is frightened it calms her to think about Marilyn Monroe. Sunny knows all about Marilyn's childhood, the foster homes, the uncles who fondled her breasts, kissed her seven-year-old nipples, and got hard. Then Marilyn knew she was a bad girl. She would always be a bad girl. It was like being at a carnival, a private carnival, just for her. There were balloons and streamers, party hats and birthday cakes with chocolate frosting and her name written in a neon pink. And no one could tell her no. She had liked to think about Marilyn Monroe when they were driving in the van between gigs. The band was in its final incarnation then. Sunny was already pregnant, and they were called Pagan Night.

When Dalton asks her what she's thinking and she says, "Nothing," she is really imagining winter and how she is certain there won't be enough to eat. Dalton says he'll shoot a cow. There are cows grazing outside of town, off half the dirt roads and along the banks of the river. Or he'll shoot a deer, an elk, he'll trap rabbits. He's been talking to people in town, at the Rio Bar. He's traded something for the fly-fishing rig, but he still has both guns and the rifle. He'll never trade the weapons, not even for heroin, even if they could find any here.

Today, on this cool morning, Sunny has walked from the river to the zoo. It is still a yellowish morning with a soft sun. Admission is one dollar, but the woman in the booth knows her and has started to simply wave her in.

Sunny passes through a gate near a willow and she would like to name the baby Willow. It would be an omen that he would survive the winter. Then she is entering the zoo, holding her baby without a name. She sits with her baby near the swan pond until someone gives her a quarter, a sandwich, a freshly purchased bag of popcorn. They simply hand it to her.

She has memorized each animal, bird, and fish in this miniature zoo. The birds stand by mossy waterfalls of the sort she imagines adorn the swimming pools of movie stars. She sits nursing her baby that she is pretending is named Willow. If anyone asks, and she knows no one will, she is prepared to say, his name is Willow.

Later, she stands in a patch of sun by an exhibit featuring a glassed-in bluish pool that should contain a penguin or a seal, but is empty. It smells derelict, harsh and sour with something like the residue of trapped wind and the final thoughts of small mammals as they chew off their feet and bleed to death. You can walk down a flight of stairs and look through the glass, but nothing is swimming. She knows. She has climbed down twice.

Sunny likes to look at what isn't there in the caged water whipped by sun. This is actually the grotto that is most full, with its battered streams of light like hieroglyphics, a language in flux, lost in shifting ripples.

She pauses in front of the golden eagle. It will not look at her, even when she whistles. The information stenciled to the cage says the golden eagle can live thirty years, longer than many movie stars, longer than Hendrix and Janis and Jim Morrison and James Dean. This particular bird will probably outlive her.

Sunny is thinking about how hungry she is when

someone offers her half a peanut-butter-and-jelly sandwich. Actually, the woman has her child do this, reach out a baby arm to her as if she is now some declawed beast you could let your kid near.

Her own baby is wrapped in her shawl, the same shawl she had once laid across the sofa in the living room of her apartment in San Francisco. She had gone there to study modern dancing, tap, and ballet. Her father wanted her to go to nursing school. If she went to nursing school, her father could believe she had finally forgotten. He could conclude that she was well and whole, and he could sleep without pills. His ulcer would disappear, he could take communion again.

Sunny took singing lessons and began to meet men with rock-and-roll bands. Nursing school became white and distant. It became a sort of moon you could put between your teeth and swallow. She stopped envisioning herself in a starched cotton uniform with a stethoscope around her neck. What she wanted now was to smoke grass and hash and opium and stare out the window at Alcatraz. What she wanted to do was sniff powder drawn in lines across a wide square of mirror she kept on the side of the sofa, like a sort of magic screen where you could watch your face change forever.

Now, at the zoo, she stands on the wood slats surrounding the fishpond filled with keepers, twenty- and twenty-five- and thirty-inch rainbow trout. This is what keepers look like. On yellow Sundays she and Dalton and the baby walk across the railroad trestle over the Snake River. But Dalton will never catch a fish this big.

She was afraid the first time they crossed the bridge. She froze with fear and Dalton had to grab her hand. He hadn't touched her body since the baby was born. He had to pull her along. The bridge was higher than she thought. And the river was rushing underneath like a sequence of waves, but faster and sharper, without breath or cycles, and she was holding the baby. That day she was secretly calling the baby Sunday. And she was cradling Sunday with one arm and Dalton was holding her other hand, pulling her through the yellow. He was also holding the fishing rod he'd somehow procured at the Rio Bar, traded somebody something for. She is beginning to think it was her black leather jacket with the studs on the cuffs, the special studs sewed on by a woman in Portland who claimed she was a gypsy.

Dalton must think she won't need her leather jacket in winter. He isn't considering what she'll need in winter. Maybe they won't still be in Idaho. Maybe they won't still be together. And the bridge was wider than she at first imagined. It was like a small pier with its set of two railroad tracks down the center, one thinner, the other fatter, one unused set covered with rust. The bridge was made from railroad ties and there were gaps between them where a foot could get caught, something small could fall through. Dalton said, "Make a pattern. Step every other one. Don't look down." That's what she did, stepped every other one, didn't look down, but still she could hear the river in a kind of anguish beneath her and she was shaking.

"It's an abandoned bridge, isn't it?" she asked Dalton.

The first few times he said yes, but when they had crossed the fourth time, he said no. She stopped, found herself staring into sun. "What do you mean?" she demanded.

"Look at the rails. The larger set are clean. Trains do this." He pointed at the tracks. "Or they'd be covered with rust."

"What if the train came now? As we were crossing?" she finally asked.

"There are beams every twenty feet," Dalton pointed to a kind of metal girder. "We'd hang on the side until it passed."

She tries to imagine herself standing on the girder, holding the baby that in her mind is named Sunday in one of her arms. She cannot conceive of this. Instead she remembers, suddenly, a story Dalton once told her years ago, before they had gone on the road, when they first recited their secret information to each other, their collection of shame, where they were truly from, what had happened, what was irrevocable.

Dalton told her about a night in high school when he had been drinking beer with his friends. Perhaps it was spring. They had been drinking since dawn and now it was after midnight. It was Ohio. That's where Dalton was from. His friends had wandered down to the train station. His best friend had tried to hop a train. Johnny Mohawk. That's what they called him, Mohawk, because he said he was part Indian. Johnny Mohawk tried to hop a train and fell. It ran over him, amputating both legs, his right arm and half of his left.

"He was so drunk, that's what saved him," Dalton explained. It must have been later. They were riding in a tour bus. They had an album out and the company had given them a roadie, a driver, and a bus. Outside was neon and wind and houses you didn't want to live in. "He was so drunk, he didn't feel it," Dalton was saying. "If he'd been more awake, the shock would have killed him."

Dalton glanced out the window, at some in-between stretch of California where there were waist-high grasses and wild flowers and a sense of too much sun, even in the darkness. She asked him what happened. She tried to imagine Johnny Mohawk but she could not. Her mind refused to accommodate the brutal lack of symmetry, would produce only words like *tunnel* and *agony, suffocate* and *scream.* Even if she had gone to nursing school, even if she went right now, enrolled in the morning, she could do nothing about Johnny Mohawk. It would always be too late.

"It was the best thing ever happened to him," Dalton said. "He was on his way to becoming a professional drunk. Like his father. Like his uncles and inbred cousins. After the accident, he got a scholarship to State. They gave him a tutor and a special car. Now he's an engineer for an oil company."

Sunny thinks about Johnny Mohawk as she stands in

the zoo, in front of a grotto with grassy sides and a sleeping male and female lion. Their cage seems too small to contain them if they wanted to do anything other than sleep in the damp green grass. She wonders what would happen if she fell in, over the low metal bar.

Near her, a pregnant woman with three blond daughters, each with a different colored ribbon in her long yellow hair, tells her two-year-old, "Don't you climb up on that bar now. You fall in, there'd be no way to get you out. That hungry old lion would eat you right up."

Sunny feels the baby in her arms, how heavy it is, how it could so easily slide from her, through the bar, into the grassy grotto. She could never retrieve it. No one would expect her to.

Then she is walking past the one zebra. When Dalton asks her if she wants to talk about anything, she shakes her head, no. She is considering how filled each no is, glittering and yellow. Each no is a miniature carnival, with curled smiles and balloons on strings and a profusion of names for babies. And in this no are syllables like *willow* and *cottonwood* and *shadow* and *Johnny Mohawk*. And in this no is the railroad trestle above one hundred thousand rainbow trout.

Sunny's favorite exhibit is the snow leopard. It is strange that a zoo in a tiny town should have such an animal. They are so rare. She reads what the snow leopard eats, mammals and birds. Its social life is solitary. How long does it live? Twenty-five years. Not quite long enough to see its first record go platinum. And it isn't really asleep on the green slope behind its grid of bars as much as it is simply turned away. Perhaps it is thinking about the past, remembering, and on its lip is something that isn't quite a smile. Or perhaps it is simply listening to the birds.

There are always birds when they cross the railroad trestle on Sunday, the Snake below them, the bald eagles and blue herons and swallows and robins, orioles and magpies in the air near their shoulders. And there is no schedule for the train. She's called Union Pacific five times, waited for the man in charge to come back from vacation, to come back from the flu, to be at his desk, and there is no way to predict when the train runs over this particular trestle. It's a local. It gets put together at the last moment, no one knows when.

When they cross the bridge on Sunday she is obsessively listening for trains. And there are so many birds, fat robins, unbelievably red, and what look like pink-and-white swallows, and orioles the yellow of chalk from fourth grade when she got an A and her teacher let her write the entire spelling list for the week on the blackboard. And ducks and Canada geese and loons, all of them stringing their syllables across the afternoon, hanging them near her face like a kind of party streamer. The baby is named Sunday or Sometimes and she feels how heavy it is, how it could just drop from her arms.

It has become obvious that these fishing Sundays are not about catching trout. It's a practice for something else entirely, for leaving, for erasure, silence, and absence. She understands now. It's the end of July. She won't be able to feed the baby from her body indefinitely, or walk through town all day looking for trash cans where she can deposit the diapers she has used over and over again.

Now it is time to rehearse. They are involved in a new show with an agenda they don't mention. It's a rehearsal for abandoning the baby. She practices leaving it on the bank, walking fifty steps away, smoking a cigarette. Then she rushes back to retrieve it, to press it against her. If she simply took a slightly longer path from the bank, permitted herself to smoke a joint, a third or fourth cigarette, she might not remember exactly where she placed the baby, not with all the foliage, the vines and brush, bushes and trees, the whole bank an ache of greenery. Something could have interceded, a sudden aberration in the river current or perhaps a hawk. She wouldn't be blamed.

In the children's petting zoo, a gray rabbit mounts a

white one. Another white rabbit eats from a bowl. They eat and mate, eat and mate. In the winter, Dalton says he'll shoot a deer. He's made a deal with somebody at the Rio Bar, something about sharing and storing. There are always cattle, fish, rabbits, beaver and otter that can be trapped.

During the day, Dalton says he's working on songs. He still has both guitars. He can only write music when the baby isn't crying or coughing. She wants to name the baby Music or Tears. She wants to name the baby Bay. She remembers the apartment they had with the view of the bridge, the way at midnight the wind felt like a sort of scalded blue. It was when everything seemed simultaneously anesthetized and hot. It was a moment she remembers as happy.

"It's not time to name it," Dalton said. He was strumming his twelve-string guitar. He said many African tribes didn't name a baby until it had survived an entire year. Dalton looked at her and smiled. His lips reminded her of Marilyn Monroe.

That's when she realized each day would have to be distinct and etched. She licks the baby's face. She sits on a bench in the sun at the zoo by a pond with a mossy waterfall in the center. There are swans in this pond. She closes her eyes and smells the baby and decides to name him Swan. She kisses his cheek and whispers in his ear, "Your name is Swan. Your name is Moss. Your name is Bye-Bye."

"What are you thinking?" Dalton asks. It was during the storm two weeks ago. He was drinking tequila. Rain struck the van and she thought of rocks and bullets and time travel.

"Nothing," she replied.

Wind. Hidden networks. The agenda that sparks. You know how night feels without candles, without light bulbs, maps, schedules. This is what we do not speak of. Bye-bye-bye, baby. Bye-bye-bye.

Every day Dalton says he's going to write songs while she is gone. He has a joint in his mouth, curled on his side in the back of the van on a ridge above the Snake River where they now live. He has a bottle of vodka tucked into his belt. The vodka is gone when she comes back. Sunny has to knock over and over against the side of the van, has to kick it with her foot, has to shout his name, until he wakes up.

Each day must be separate, an entity, like a species, a snow leopard, a zebra, or a rainbow trout. Each one with a distinct evolution and morphology, niches, complex accidents. Last Sunday she smoked a joint and drank tequila as they crossed the river on the railroad ties. She has a pattern, left foot, skip one with the right, left foot, skip one with the right, don't look down.

She knows it will happen on a Sunday, perhaps next Sunday. Dalton will say, "Come over, look at this."

"I can't. I'm feeding the baby," she will answer.

"Put it down a second," he'll say. "You've got to see this."

She'll place the baby in the center of soft weeds. She'll follow the sound of his voice, find Dalton on the bank with a great trout, twenty inches, thirty inches long. It will be their keeper and she will bend down, help him pull it in. Her feet will get wet. She will use her hat for a net, her red hat printed with the words *Wyoming Centennial 1990*. The seconds will elongate, the minutes will spread into an afternoon, with no one counting or keeping track. When they've pulled the trout in, when they've finished the tequila, it will be dark. They will begin searching for the baby, but there will be only shadow. No one could say they were at fault. No one could say anything. No one knows about them or the baby, and the van has got at least five thousand miles left in it. They could be in New York or Florida in two days.

Perhaps it will be a Sunday when they are crossing the bridge. She'll be holding the baby named Sometimes or

Swan or Willow, and they'll have to leap onto the steel girders as the train rushes by. The baby will drop from her arms into the Snake, and it will be taken on the current like Moses.

They will never mention the falling. They will not speak of it, not once. It will just be something caught in the edge of their smile, like a private carnival that went through town and maybe you saw it once and too briefly and then it was gone.

She knows Dalton believes they are purer, more muscle and bone, closer to an archetypal winter beyond artifice. That was part of why they called the band Pagan Night. They are animals, barbarians, heathens. They are pagan and recognize this, its possibilities and what it costs. In China and India, girl children are often drowned at birth. There are fashions of surviving famines engraved on the nerves.

Maybe this Sunday they will be crossing the bridge when the train erupts from a spoil of foliage and shadow, avenues of willows and heron and orioles. Dalton will have left his guitar in the van, padlocked with his paperback myths of primitive people. Perhaps it will be a Sunday after Dalton returns from the Rio Bar with heroin. They will have cooked it up and had it that night, all night, and the next day, all day until it was finished and there was nothing left, not even in the cotton in the spoon.

When she stands on the Sunday railroad trestle she will think about ineluctable trajectories. There is a destiny to the direction and journey of all objects, stars and birds, babies and stones and rivers. Who can explain how or why that snow leopard came from Asia to reside in an obsolete grotto in a marginal farming town among barley and potato fields in southern Idaho? What shaped such a voyage, what miscalculations, what shift of wind or currents, what failure of which deity?

Sunny knows exactly what she will be thinking when it happens. There are always acres of sun and their fading.

It is all a sequence of erasures and absences. Who is to say flesh into water or flesh into rock is not a form of perfection? What of Moses on the river with an ineluctable destiny to be plucked from reeds by a princess? Perhaps on some fishing Sunday when the baby is named Swallow or Tiger and falls from her arms, someone on a distant bank will look up and say they saw the sudden ascension of a god.

near-death experiences

It was the day before Thanksgiving when Sarah was hit by the car. Gwen was talking on the telephone at the precise instant of impact. She was simultaneously wishing Jonathan's colleagues happy holidays and collecting money for a charity she was increasingly less enthusiastic about, a shelter for homeless women that advertised too aggressively.

Why were they spending funds on brochures with sentimental photographs of laughing children instead of actually feeding people? She felt duplicitous and awkward, soliciting contributions for a cause about which she felt ambivalent.

"You haven't believed in anything since Altamont," Jonathan once noted. It was not a reproach.

Gwen considers the matter of volition and how that must be factored in. After all, some women choose homelessness. Perhaps they discover it accidentally, happen to ride a bus and realize they don't actually have to exit at their regular stop. No one is watching. It's a confluence between grids, a sudden opening in shadow. They don't have to cook dinner, pick up the children, vacuum the den. They can ride until they find a grassy slope. They can sleep beneath an archive of stars. They can return to the jungle.

Some women divest themselves of answers. They don't need to read the headlines. Is it trespass or transcendence? Such women might tell you they have contrived to forget all but the subtleties of meeting and departure. They don't need to balance the checkbook. They refuse to watch their weight. They no longer require pastel in spring. They forget the date of their anniversary. It is always the same solitary moment of birds skimming across water. It is always a sky of martyrs and kidnapping. Sunset lingers like slaughter above the dried reeds. Some women choose landscape as a companion. They learn to speak without mouths.

There was a bottle of codeine cough syrup left over from their recent family bout with the flu. Gwen allowed herself one swig after each phone call. She took one now, suddenly despising the ritual of holidays, the domestic details and their repetition. She would have preferred the life of a recluse, she was thinking, just as the emergency phone call came in. Not a woman in rags on the grass beneath a freeway overpass, but perhaps a sort of middle-aged scholar.

She often considered returning to the university, not as a professor—she had resigned her position without regret soon after Sarah was born—but rather as a student. When Jonathan presented a paper or taught a seminar, she would wander through one college or another, evaluating the student housing, and imagining the three of them living in a subsidized apartment on campus.

At the University of California in Santa Cruz, the student apartments were set beneath redwood trees on a bluff overlooking the ocean, which was a glassy violet. Deer like scrawny dogs grazed between foliage. There were studios with skylights for painters. Jonathan could start his academic career in something else entirely, philosophy, perhaps, or law. She could try art. They could be undergraduates together until Sarah was ready for college. Then she and Jonathan could matriculate and move in with their daughter. They could stay indefinitely in the redwood grove with its view of deer and stalled bay the fluid blue of an ink one might choose for penning a love letter. There would be redwood flakes on the ground like cinnamon and the wind smelling of sea and mint.

"Don't ask me to apply for a position here," Jonathan had warned her. "You have that look."

Of course, Sarah wouldn't want them. That was the primary defect with her plan. Sarah would have discovered her own version of rock and roll by then. She already complained about Hendrix and Dylan. Their tastes would be completely different. There would be too much noise. That's when the emergency call interrupted.

"This is the Los Angeles Police Department. Are you Sarah's mother?" a woman asked. The voice seemed artificial, as if it was being translated from some other language and era.

"Yes. I'm Sarah's mother," Gwen said. It was an admission. "What is it?" And she knew it was very bad.

"Your daughter's been hit by a car," the voice said. "But she's all right. She's at Wilshire and Doheny."

"I'm on my way," Gwen answered.

There was a new rhythm, and she understood and entered it. It was a sort of staccato in which she delivered her memorized lines. She had a role, with gestures and words. She felt detached from herself and the room.

Then she is moving into the late November afternoon, into its slim lime shadows, into its sense of moist geranium and fern. Rain has recently fallen. There is a subtle smell of washed palms. The bushes look as if they are molting. There are transformations beside the hibiscus and the starched white azaleas like crepe. These are the subdued tropics, she thinks, but there are ambushes, tears in the fabric.

There are so many ambulances, fire trucks, and police cars that traffic has stopped moving. The sirens sound like swarms of fierce, poisoned birds. Gwen parks in a stranger's driveway and begins running. The sky is so blue it makes her face ache, she thinks her teeth may fall out. There is only motion and how she is entering it, thinking of her sister Tina.

Her sister spent her last six months putting on layers of perfume. Tina had developed a system. It began with the creams, then the perfume, and finally the mist of cologne. Tina sprayed her neck, her wrists, her clothing, and the scarf she wrapped her bald head in. Chemotherapy had made her hair fall out. It had all disappeared to the last pale strand. Her sister was swathed in loose clothing. She had finally gotten thin. And she seemed to be wearing only ritual garments, robes and kaftans, fabrics like tapestries with beaded edges. Tina carried perfume bottles with her. Tina, behind her private blue rain. Tina, veiled and elemental, on morphine the last eight weeks, opening her mouth and not speaking, spraying mist instead. Perhaps she imagined she was dissolving sapphires in the air between them.

"I never understood how simple it was. To smell lavender and vanilla. I could have stood in the kitchen and been perfectly happy. Where was I, all of my life?" her sister had asked, not rhetorically. Her sister Tina, anointing a scarf with cologne and placing the fabric in her hands. That was their last afternoon together.

"I want to give you something," Tina had said. It was raining. They were in the hospital. Her sister unwrapped the yellow silk scarf from her hairless head. She sprayed it with perfume, offered it to her, then squeezed the fabric into her fingers. "Close your eyes," her sister commanded.

Gwen shut her eyes. She was thinking one could drown in clarities. The air was morphine green. It was a sort of aquarium. She smelled the hospital, its relentless glare, its greasy too-thick white light that suggested children's paint or masks. Outside were storm clouds and thunder. Her sister could not walk to the window. Her sister would never get out of bed again. Gwen thought, what is there to see, anyway, that would not break your heart? The palms, windswept and brazen, washed with surprise? Then the disguised dusk and the mime of street lights, the soft yellow pulse.

"It smells like the China Sea in autumn," Tina had said. "Though I've never been there and I don't expect I ever will." Her sister died seven hours later.

Now a crowd has gathered near the corner. A woman holding a shopping bag points at her and she hears someone say, "That must be the mother."

Gwen is running toward the ambulance when a fireman grabs her by the shoulders. He holds her in place, firmly. "We had a hell of a time getting her quiet. We can't let you in like this. You calm down first."

So, she is the mother. That's what the bystander said. And she is not calm. Now she has two facts. Jonathan has taught her the significance of observation and data one can replicate. He's a physicist.

Gwen doesn't believe in physics. Who is to say what is really plausible? Who draws the line, in what phase of firm green shadow, in what arroyo of chartreuse? Who is in charge of the interplay?

In the beginning they talked about physics, and she thought she understood infinity. It was a state where all attributes are random and grace is as possible as cataclysm. Gwen has come to think it nauseating to contemplate infinity, to view every possibility as being actual. Just considering the city of Los Angeles is sickening. Or other continents.

Once, just after their marriage, they attended a scientific conference in Moscow. It was winter and at the conclusion of the symposium they took a train to Leningrad, and then Kiev. Each week was a food theme. First cherries, canned cherries at every breakfast and lunch for seven consecutive days. Monday became blueberries, fourteen meals, across thousands of aching white miles, yogurt and hard black bread and blueberries. The third week was pineapple.

In the snow, beside locked cathedrals, beside looted and forbidden churches with broken windows, were boxes with the overly representational tropical symbols of fruit and flower petals pasted on the cardboard. This fruit came from Cuba. It was enough of a juxtaposition, the lurid yellow decorated boxes almost buried in the deep snow. There were implications enough to consider, without positing worlds even more hysterical or bereft.

"Are you calm now?" the fireman asked. "Are you ready?"

Gwen is the mother and she is supposed to be ready. She is thinking about physics. She often asked Jonathan what there was to discover, after all? That we are moving slower than we thought, personally and globally? That we are barbarians with lace panties, machine guns, and charge cards? In the airports and train stations of all the capitals, there are booths selling black strapless bras and Pearl Jam. We are barely crawling across the tiles, the cement, the lobbies, dragging our suitcases and bad childhoods with us. We are much too slow for our lives. Daddy is yanking us by the arm. We have screamed our throats raw and help didn't come. Where is the divorce, the inheritance? How much time to fill between here and the morphine pump?

"Are you ready?" the fireman repeated. He was accustomed to this rhythm, its sequence of pause and repetition.

"Just tell me," Gwen took a deep breath. "Is she bleeding?"

"No. She's not bleeding," the fireman assured her.

Gwen climbed into the ambulance. The driver was telephoning Jonathan and they were moving. Sarah's leg was set inside a sort of enormous transparent plastic cast. It was a balloon sculpture with serious intentions. Her daughter's entire face was incredibly red. She might have been smeared with raspberry or special ritual clays. She looked inflamed, radiated, perhaps, and Gwen found herself asking, "What's wrong with your face?"

"Not my face," Sarah told her, corrected her, really. "It's my leg. Can't you see? The car ran over my leg."

There was a problem with seeing, Gwen realized later in her reconstruction of events, a problem with seeing and hearing. It began with the woman's voice on the emergency telephone call. It delivered facts flatly, efficiently. It was a sort of syllable transport system.

"She was crossing on green," the fireman said. "The guy in the Benz ran the light. You have a good girl. A smart girl. She kept her head. And she was in the right."

It's important to be in the right, no question about that. Go on green. Stop on red. The laws of thermodynamics. The way you are obligated to exit the vehicle at your regular stop, pick up the cleaning, insist the children finish their homework, practice the piano. You are not permitted a moment that elongates, stalls, offers an alternative morphology. A moment when you recognize you can have everything if you continue past your regular stop. If you dare, you can possess mesas, arroyos, dynasties of charged magenta sand. You can hear the night howl. You can howl with it.

In between are rules. There is the way porcelain plates fall and break in a 6.7 earthquake. There is the way Jonathan explained infinity to Sarah. It was the subject of her sixth-grade extra-credit science report. They sat together in the study, the computer making its windy useless hum, screen filled with a listless fireworks. It was the sound of the twentieth century, an artificial wind, tinny and abortive. Time passing grayly, shabbily. Jonathan and Sarah were talking about alternative worlds and listening to them made her dizzy.

"Are you disputing quantum mechanics?" Sarah demanded. She glanced at her father, as if to say, Mother is whimsical, foolish.

"Yes," she had replied and looked out the window. It was a day of expectation. Beyond the sun filtering through the ecru lace curtains there could be a slow sequence of bells, perhaps, or two bridges where she had never before seen them. There could be a river with reeds, a bend with shadow, lime, deep, as if it had been there for years. Such a river could teach you something. You could stand on its shore and turn in circles until you found resolution in a bank of parched grass.

"How do you justify that?" Sarah asked. Her daughter was holding a Magic Marker. She was making a diagram on a pasteboard. She was president of the science club.

"I think the universe is immensely vast but ultimately finite," Gwen said. There would be a river at the end of all the worlds, a river like agate behind the insult of obscure smoke. There would be geranium, fern and sweet william. It would be a perpetual spring scented with terror.

"Well, if there isn't infinity, what's at the end of the universe?" Sarah's tone was insistent. She glanced at Jonathan. They would humor her.

"At the end of the universe? A McDonald's and a parking lot," Gwen said.

"Then what?" Sarah stared at her.

"Then the final mall. And a sort of outdoor warehouse where a raw wind blows giant stacks of non-fire-resistant pajamas. The ones taken off the American market and sold in the Third World. Then the piles of blankets subject to spontaneous combustion. And the boxes of baby formula without the right vitamins. And the medicines with the known side effects, the ones that twist bones and incite cancer," Gwen said.

She wanted a cigarette. Gwen had stopped smoking when she became pregnant. Recently she had begun to consider making a conscious decision to start smoking again. Friends would stop inviting them for dinner. She would become a pariah, a woman who consorted with flame. Then she wouldn't have to ask for contributions to charities that spent their funds on self-promotion

"Then what?" Sarah persisted, showing her father how

smart she was, how verbal and scientific, how determined.

"Then you fall asleep and there are asters and lupine and larkspur everywhere," Gwen said. "Janis Joplin is singing 'Summertime' and all the people you've loved and lost sit in a circle near you."

"That's my Berkeley girl," Jonathan said.

Gwen envisioned the end of the universe as a sequence of blue, fragile and translucent like the skin of infants. It was the blue of a stamp fading on a passport. We are given documents at birth. Life is a visa. At the end, one final port of exit.

"You mean she's right?" Sarah glared at her father.

"Your mother is always both right and not even close. You know that," Jonathan said. Then he had kissed her and she thought of the cherries all week in Russia, then the blueberries. In memory, the snow was fragrant and bruised.

"Am I going to die?" Sarah is asking. Her voice seems crushed.

They are riding in an ambulance. She cannot hear the siren. Sarah's face is the color of pomegranates and strawberries. She is not bleeding. She is a good girl.

"Of course not," Gwen answers.

She is holding her daughter's hand. They are hurtling down boulevards, through intersections. Gwen thinks of her sister, the last days, when Tina's mouth would form shapes but she could not decipher them. There were secret architectures in the room, fragments, invisible origami. Tina kept spraying perfume into the air, onto her black satin nightgown and the sheets that were her own bedding.

She had brought her own linens to the hospital, her childhood quilt. The sheets were a floral print, purples and magentas and the browns of dried blood. Her sister was lying on a ruined garden. Wind was blowing. Everything was cold. She felt the ocean was coming in the windows, with a fine salty dust, a fragrance composed from the residue of sunken cargoes. She could smell what she thought was moon.

Everything was veiled in azure. Her sister was behind a mist of powdered lilacs. Tina was speaking but no words came out of her mouth. Gwen realized that language is limited by the heart, by its capacity for grief and ambiguity. Experience makes us mute. At such junctures an honest woman would bang her head against rocks until she was bloody.

"Am I broken?" Sarah asks.

"No. Just shaken up. You'll be fine," Gwen knows to say.

Outside the ambulance are streets she once lived on and in, where her multitude of former selves inhabited houses and lofts that are now apartment buildings, are now Indian restaurants, air perpetually the yellow of curry. She lived with men who might now be dead, literally, painters and actors, dead and buried and she never got funeral announcements, never received property condemned notifications.

The city is inhabited by her former incarnations. There are earlier selves so distant she wouldn't be able to pick out those other Gwens from a line-up. We are like virulent viruses, she thinks, subject to constant mutation. It's emotional mutation, and in the end they need to identify us by our dental records.

Her sister invariably let all of her plants die. Tina was a conceptual gardener. She found the actual work of tending to be tedious. It was only in the last six months that she developed a capacity to nurture, to be patient with dirt and stems, to enter into covenants with the ground.

"I could have had children, after all," Tina realized, surprised. "I would have known what to do."

Tina had already lost her hair. She had gone to Paris, Rome, and Jerusalem wearing a silk turban. She sailed and scuba dived in Maui. She stayed two weeks in Hong Kong. She spent her savings on travel.

"Everyone should live like they have cancer," Tina advised her. "People don't know how to live. And they don't know how to die."

Her sister sold stock and had flowers delivered to her house every morning, bouquets of roses and peonies. She planted a garden and studied it, pruned and watered and coaxed it. She got down on her knees and opened her fingers to green.

"I'm going to meet the dogs at the gate," Tina had said, shears in her hand that afternoon. "I'm running up with a soup bone and a machete. Nothing will surprise me."

Now the ambulance is pulling into the underground emergency-room entrance. She came through this door to give birth to Sarah twelve years ago. She is still holding Sarah's hand. Their flesh feels fused. "This is the only time we'll ever get to Cedars without a parking problem," she tells her daughter. Sarah doesn't smile.

Her daughter has been taken to a partitioned area in the emergency room where she is examined by a tired-looking female doctor. The vital signs are normal. There is a slight fever, that is all. Then Sarah is placed on a gurney and wheeled into x-ray.

Gwen is holding a plastic bag that contains Sarah's belongings, the clothing she was wearing and what she was carrying, her gray gym sweat shirt and pants, the change from her pockets, her backpack crammed with books. There are miscellaneous items, including a rabbit's-foot key chain she has never seen before and Sarah's antique gold locket that is not supposed to leave the house under any circumstances.

Gwen considers the reports of near-death experiences she has read about in tabloids. She has always been interested in these accounts. The recurrent theme of white lights. The implication that life is a sequence of pearls strung together, the moments so clear they are almost three-dimensional. The sense that there are random resurrections, inexplicable and continual, just as there are tumors, fires, and plague. We are stuck down. We are risen. There is another competing logic, more elegant and subtle than what science knows.

She has her own theories of plausibility. It is even possible the sightings of dead celebrities contain some element of truth. If one subscribes to concepts of infinity, there are worlds where the dead are still living. Perhaps there are junctures of confluence where one can look between worlds. Perhaps there are camouflaged bridges, sunken corridors, black holes in the fabric you find by opening a window or a door.

Janis Joplin is not dead. She did not overdose on heroin in a Los Angeles motel, falling to the floor with such force that she broke her nose. That's only the official story. Perhaps Janis managed to disappear from one grid to another. Janis is really living in the San Fernando Valley. She is completely happy, transcendent. She has three children and sings in the choir on Sunday. She is married to a fireman and their fighting is notorious. She knocks back Southern Comfort in the Baptist church parking lot, flagrantly, as if no one can see her, as if she were veiled in white light. She wipes her mouth with her hand while they gossip about her clothes and alcohol consumption and how extravagant her jewelry is. There is speculation about her penchant for feathers and how she pays her bills. There is a complete absence of fact. Whenever she is asked, she gives a different name. Some know her as Sherry or Joan, Terry, Melissa and Diane.

"How is she?" Jonathan asks, voice measured, soft. His words are a gauze, a white cloth he could wrap her in.

Gwen has watched him approach through the gluey-white corridor, his face stern and pale. It looks fixed, rocky, paralyzed. In an alternative world, they have come to Cedars Sinai Medical Center because he has had a stroke. Later, she will push him in a wheelchair along the boardwalk. They will age together in the company of tamed waves breaking on shore like a sequence of sung notes in a musical scale. She will push him up to a bluff where they can watch waves break and foam before they hear the sound. There will be the interval between cause and effect like a perfect blue free-fall, like confetti drifting in wind.

"She seems OK. She's in x-ray," Gwen says.

Then Sarah is in the corridor, in a wheelchair with them. Sarah is wearing a hospital gown. Nothing is broken. The doctor notes one fist-sized bruise on Sarah's thigh. It looks like a claw mark.

A nurse tells Sarah that she can get dressed. She is going to be released. In a partitioned area, Gwen helps her daughter back into her blue jeans, her blue-and-yellow flannel shirt. Then Sarah is wheeled out of the emergency room. She looks abnormally squat, agitated, and defeated.

"Do I have to go to school tomorrow?" Sarah asks for the third time.

"No," Jonathan answers.

Gwen watches him walk down the driveway, toward the street where he has parked his car. He is a tall man with a white face, carrying a plastic bag of objects taken from the body of his struck-down child. He has not had a stroke. Sarah was born in this hospital and her sister died in this hospital. Gwen believes the universe is not infinite but rather almost incalculably large. At the core is Cedars Sinai Medical Center, where she has been hospitalized numerous times, been cut and sewed, scraped and opened, biopsied and survived. This current Gwen and her former selves, all of them still somehow lingering here, like tributaries in rivers that empty into a central sea.

"What are you looking at?" Sarah asks.

Gwen cannot begin to answer. She thinks she is searching for Tina. She held her sister's hand and it reminded her of an orange. It was solid, but complex, clearly a container. She would close her eyes and trace Tina's skin, surprised by the tiny ridges and imperfections.

It made her think that death was even more insidious than she imagined.

She envisioned sticking her thumbnail into Tina's skin and peeling the first layer as one did an orange, sliding under the rind, then the simultaneous feel of the damp pulp and the smell that was Los Angeles in August, any backyard or alley. It was the scent of their childhood, citrus in heat and dust, oleander and stucco and a cut on your leg and the sun setting, finally, in a smear the color of iodine.

The oranges hanging above the streets were a sort of promise, a sequence of lanterns in the afternoon, marking their passage, defining their childhood the way buoys outlined the shallows of the bay. Oranges hung like secret eyes above the boulevards, camouflaged behind their indifferent pastel, which was like neon washed in acid, the life leached out. You were watched, but without interest.

Gwen kissed her sister's hand, surprised not by the sweetness—the oranges along the boulevards of their childhood Los Angeles were never sweet—but by something unexpected and rancid. It was like touching a bad dream with your tongue. Perhaps it was from the morphine or the chemotherapy or the cancer itself.

She imagined biting into her sister's hand and sucking the venom out. She thought, we carry our childhood with us. We caress it with our mouths. We marry it. There are no other possible points of resolution. The compass is broken. We are always circling and we circle until we drop. We are where we started. We are always home.

Now her daughter is sitting in a wheelchair, a little girl with slumped shoulders and eyes red from crying. A fireman has given her a candy bar and she is eating it, without permission, in complete disregard for her retainers. Jonathan is driving up slowly and she takes a deep breath.

The day smells, somehow, of opal. It seems polished, fluorescent, precious. She thinks of near-death experiences. It seems that after such an accident there should be a clarification, a distillation, a coalescing of specifics. She asks Sarah if she was aware of anything extraordinary.

"You mean besides like two thousand pounds on my leg?" Sarah is surprised, almost offended. "I thought that was pretty unusual."

Gwen helps her daughter from the wheelchair and into the car. Jonathan has opened the door. Sarah is limping slightly. One of her shoes is torn.

"I know what you need," Gwen announces suddenly, inspired.

"You have no idea what I need," Sarah says, mostly to herself. "You need this," Gwen insists, extracting a bottle from her purse and spraying it on the side of Sarah's flannel shirt as she squirms away. The car fills with what might be larkspur or delphinium. Her sister was saturating rooms with lavender colognes. She was trying to say God has a blue uncertain hand. He plays dice with your life and his hand shakes like an old man's with Parkinson's.

The car smells of revelation, of a central fact that gleams like bleached violets. She understands precisely what Tina wanted to tell her. At the end of the universe, after the last parking lot, after the last crack house, after the last bruised infant in the final trailer park, everything looks like Santa Monica Bay in autumn. It is cleansed past bone, freed of insomnia and wounds. You see beneath the false outer layer. You can see the pulse. There's a church nearby. The choir is singing. One woman is scratching at the soft late afternoon with her voice. She is strangling on bourbon and magnolias. She's eaten petals dipped in flame. This is the sign. Now we put our bags down. Now we unpack.

She is still holding Sarah's hand. At best, we offer our loved ones fragrant rags. We are all homeless women, crash victims, chance survivors. We are always crossing invisible bridges, losing our lockets, waiting for planes. We pretend we know where we're going. We are attending to our watches, springing forward, falling back, aching for lamplight, a pier, an alley or a mooring we recognize. We all need a cot for the night. We set up improvised and temporary camp. We sleep beneath an assault of stars. We sleep on the edge of the jungle.

It is her daughter's first near-death experience, and they are driving along a boulevard named for a saint, their hands fused, into a dusk Gwen recognizes. It is the end of November in Los Angeles and it is as it must be, a communion of transitory lilac.

a conjunction of dragon ladies

He leaves her in the hotel with the three-bridged view of the bay. He is interviewing a scientist she always thought she wanted to meet. They've planned it this way, to be in San Francisco on their anniversary. They have managed this precise conjunction of time and place for five con-secutive years. It is the room where they fell in love.

He asks again at the door, turning back, if she won't change her mind and join him. She declines with a slight smile.

"Maybe I'll take a short walk," she says. "Taste the wind." She is casual.

"So you are going out?" Evan realizes. He recognizes there are intricacies in this wind-tasting, something with spices or pieces of tin or sail perhaps. When he studies her face, she realizes her skin in a sequence of leaves he sifts at the bottom of teacups.

"Maybe briefly," Caroline tells him. "But I'll be back by two."

When he is gone, the silence elongates and deepens. She thinks of aquariums. Or places where entire carcasses are mounted, the heads of elk and deer and pronged sheep. Or entire bear, standing upright, with their claws petrified on slabs of simulated rock.

When they first came to this room it was sunset and

the city seemed subtle, rose and gold, open and subdued, racked with a slow fever of clouds. The Berkeley hills were pastel. She considered the possibility that this was the bay of deliverance. Evan could pour salt on her wounds, they would be erased, pulled out in the current running under the orange bridge and ending on a beach in China.

Later the lights along the boulevards looked like molecules of neon or the pulse of drugs in a vein. She thought they looked like love or time travel. And she knew she had found the illuminated perimeter, the wires with their gold electric.

Now Caroline notices that the lamps on the bedside tables have been changed. They were a floral, a leaf like an autumn maple. Today they are a suggestion of mauve. And the ottoman from the window sofa has been removed. It has been ten minutes since her husband left. She has visualized the individual events of his departure, the elevator and the arrival of the taxi cab and how it turned the corner.

She puts on her black leather jacket, a blue Dodgers baseball cap, and mirrored sunglasses. Then she is crossing the carpeted lobby with its slight implication of buds. She is walking up a hill, two hills, three with the smell of coffee and slow sunlight across anonymous waves.

The hills across the bay remind her of brown discarded flesh. Or abandoned women, she thinks, exiled, of no use anymore. Some man sent them away.

She crests a hill and has somehow arrived on Vallejo Street in Chinatown. People are congregated on the sidewalk just ahead of her. They are staring at a point moving along the edge of the gutter. Caroline stands near them and looks where they do.

A tiny Asian woman with black windblown hair like a sort of fishing net hanging down her back is screaming. She gestures with her little arms and spits, furious. Caroline thinks it is part of a street-theater performance.

Later there will be a juggler and a mime and a boy willing to sketch your face for change. Then she sees the three policemen. They are handcuffing the woman, who is shrieking like a bird.

Caroline considers birds that return, obsessive swallows, perhaps, drawn back yearly to their walled adobe mission where they hear the bells and do not understand them. There are bits of prayers rising from cactus and dust. Or perhaps sound can be a kind of hieroglyphic one can comprehend by the act of receiving air.

The miniature woman who is not an actress is yelling in English and Chinese. She tries to bite the policeman. She lunges at his arm with her mouth. The policeman is Oriental and tall, perhaps six feet. He seems amused. He asks the screaming woman's mother, "Can you handle her?" He has rested one of his hands on his gun. He is smiling.

The mother says, "No." She shakes her head vigorously from side to side as if to clear it. This is a city of fog, after all, and camouflaged dangers. The mother is wearing a red Forty-Niners' sweatshirt. She is holding a broom. She turns her back from the street where her daughter is howling and begins to sweep the curb with wide circular motions.

"Then it's back to the hospital," the large amused policeman says. He nods vaguely to the crowd, simultaneously recognizing and dismissing them. There has been a spectacle of some sort, but it has passed.

The wild-haired woman has been lifted into a police van. Caroline can still hear her voice. Wailing is issuing forth from a kind of vent in the side of the van. She is a bird woman, Caroline decides, transforming the vehicle into a kind of aviary, transmitting her version of events through the metal mesh. It is a frenzied transmission. And now someone replies.

It is an old Chinese woman standing directly next to her, a woman with one wide braid like a gray snake wrapped around her head and vast continents of rouge on her cheeks. "It's brutality, brutality," the old woman shouts.

Caroline is interested in this. "But her mother doesn't want her," she explains. She gestures toward the woman with the broom. It is essential to clarify this point.

The woman with the braid shakes her head. "It's wrong, wrong," she tells her. "Don't they know? Sometimes a woman has to go traveling." Caroline can feel the old woman's fingers through her leather jacket. "Sometimes women just have to go traveling, yes?"

Caroline considers this. We are all alone, she thinks, encoded, veiled within our intricate fictions. The rouged woman is looking up at her, expecting something. "Yes," Caroline agrees. "Sometimes women must go traveling."

Caroline can still hear the tiny woman screaming through the mesh of the police van behind her. The woman with hair like a fishing net, and now she has been trapped. She will be taken to a dockside where she will be bartered or sold by the pound. And when Caroline glances at her watch she is startled that twenty minutes have already passed.

Caroline walks faster, hearing the rhythm her boots make on the sidewalk, striking the pavement. She might be trying to hammer something into the ground, a series of signals that burrow under and echo like gongs. Somewhere a woman is looking out a bay window and she will hear.

Ducks and chickens hang in the shop windows. They look lacquered and molten, like they've been tortured. Now you could eat them or wear them as beads. We are all barbarians, Caroline thinks. We stand in the gutters of narrow streets decorated with defiled fowl red as condensed dragons and our mothers let men handcuff us and lock us inside metal aviaries on wheels. Later we will be plucked and exhibited, sold into slavery, into brothels, into restraints and tranquilizers. All women know this as the price for traveling. In between, we study the clocks on our wrists. They are the bands in a network of imperatives. We say we will be back at two and we are.

Caroline pauses in front of a vegetable market. There are stacks of what might be cucumbers but they are a flagrant purple and she knows they did not come from the bay, the ocean would not permit or absolve such a configuration.

It is a shop of aberrations, and Caroline is surprised by her impulse. She wants to smell it all, touch it all. Can these unknown orbs and spheres really feel as they look— painted, cool and smooth as a stone the sea has intimately polished? Of course there are forms of knowledge that can only be imparted through the fingertips, certain complexities that are partially tactile, that must be traced with pieces of the body. Some truths involve rituals of neurons.

The shop is scented from the dust-colored ovals she recognizes as roots. They have dug in. They know. And it occurs to her that this is what you must hold to your ear. This is what could give you the blueprint and the history, not the shell, which is empty and tells you only its name, over and over. It will not even reveal the port from which it first accidentally came or the storm that was an ambush. It will not tell you the reasons.

She is drawn to a store with grotesque poultry stuck on hooks near the windows. These bodies resemble shrunken, suspended dragons. There are numerous strings on which the backs of the webbed feet of chickens have been tied. There are the organs she cannot identify. It is possible there was a sequence of predawn autopsies. And these matted fistlike curling mounds cannot be livers. They are too big. She is certain. She can still trust her sense of proportion in objects and their physical orderings.

She crosses the street, sensing a point of entry. She stops, breathless, in front of a fish market. There are moments when her heart seems to stall, when she can't get air into her lungs. It is a form of being becalmed. This is how she imagines asthma and emphysema must be. She has decided her breathlessness is a reaction to certain forms of startlement. For instance, she feels this way when she sees her name handwritten on an envelope. It is an unexpected intimacy, a kind of violation.

The fish on their beds of ice have their eyes open. They have ridges that have turned red and a vague odor that might be an attribute of sunlight and fog, nothing intrusive. She is trying to breathe and the air is deceptive and subtle. It feels powdered, as if from parchment and impermanence. Nothing could stain her in such a place. Then she breathes easily.

She is standing on a narrow crowded street with a Spanish name. There is a sudden noise and a white truck stops, two men slide open the huge back door and the floor of the vehicle is filled with carcasses. Men unload mounds of beef with a hook, entire halves of animals. Caroline can see their feet dangling over the shoulder of the men carrying them.

There is a theme of feet here, she recognizes. The feet of chickens suspended in windows and the feet still attached to the bones on the sides of beef. Here hooves and claws are not discarded. She watches two men with hooks enter a room where other men begin cutting the half-animals into pieces with handsaws. A portable tape deck on the long table where the strips of meat are being assembled is playing Tom Petty and the Heartbreakers. She has this tape in her car in Los Angeles.

She turns the corner and comes to a street of fish markets. The fish are a dark mysterious gray like the essence of late afternoon waters in autumn. Their mouths are uniformly open, as if in a collective chant. Or perhaps it is a recognition of something beyond horror, transcendent, some concept all breathing things know absolutely at the end.

Caroline notices that their eyes are bulging and they are all facing in the same direction. This must be where God really is, she thinks. If a woman had a compass at a time like this, if a woman had a globe or a map, she could tell you where Mecca really should be, where to dig for oil, where to plant the crops, the way to lay out trees in orchards, the direction pregnant women should face on feast days, and of course where to bury loved ones and where to pray.

There is an assertion of order and purpose in the arrangement of these fish. Someone laid them out as if they were separate entities, individuals. Someone stopped and deciphered the details of their morphologies. These are corpses and their deaths have been orchestrated. Reasons rise from the early afternoon slabs of ice, signals with direction. It's a matter of angles and knowing precisely when to listen.

Nearby, in a sort of trench or sink, crabs are fanning themselves with their claws. They have turned the water blue. Pieces of fish resemble slices of watermelon. And she must have crossed a street and climbed another hill because now there are shelves with fruits, stacks of purple grapes, piles of gourds that look like yams but aren't. She touches the side of what might be a yellow pear and is surprised by the chill. She turns and walks back into the sun and a street of bakeries and bells and birds, and suddenly there are clouds above her.

It is one o'clock, that is what the cathedral bells above the almond cookies and pale yellow honey cakes are saying. She has one hour left, and it is not possible that she can return to the hotel on time. She is outside a huge mart filled with tea sets and dishes, and there are entire worlds to decipher in the red and purple painted flowers along the rims and borders where you might place your lips. There are litanies and sagas in the tureens shaped like fish.

She finds herself standing on a corner with a newsstand. She studies the papers in Asian scripts with colored photographs of young women across the front pages. They are wearing unnaturally red lipstick on their half-opened mouths and blue jeans with the zippers part way undone. It occurs to Caroline that they are offering their faces to the many winds in the uncountable harbors.

Always, there are these young women without blouses, with their long black hair combed partially across their breasts. This is what waits on the corners in newsstands on Stockton and Jackson Streets in San Francisco. They are what waits in San Pedro and Seattle and Taiwan, Hong Kong and Los Angeles.

Caroline considers this imaginary Chinese empire that has outgrown the literal face of maps and become internalized and diffused. She remembers the Chinese restaurants she has seen in the cities of the West, in Nevada, Idaho, and Colorado. Then she looks at her wristwatch and another five minutes have passed.

And time forms an empire, she lets herself think, walking fast. It's about invisible nets and not getting caught, like the woman who was found traveling, overt and undiminished, too far from the water, and it required three large men to subdue her, men with guns and billy clubs, walkie talkies and vans. The exposed woman with her secret net showing across her back and even her mother didn't want her.

Caroline has come to a shop with piles of what might be sticks. Perhaps they are used for cooking or in acts of magic or sex. They could be about divining or searching the future or perhaps you push them inside your body. She considers the things that look like fetuses in jars and wonders if they are connected to the unusual sticks, is there a process of manipulation, some procedure employing cause and effect?

At the bottom of a steep hill is a vast open arcade stacked with dishes and Buddhas. She was been planning to buy a tea set and a Buddha for years. She doesn't drink tea but she feels it is a taste she should acquire. She was not initiated into teas in the '60s. She didn't like their contrived exotic names and the people who drank them and talked about astrology and moving to farms. She preferred the hard edge of caffeine and people with political ideas in cafés.

It occurs to her that she miscalculated. She visualizes

herself in a kitchen lined with glistening white shelves and philodendrons. She would keep her teas for potency, serenity, and sleep in small glass jars and vials, each labeled with their lyrical names and purported attributes affixed to them by calligraphy. She could spend afternoons selecting and mixing, brewing and pouring. A time-honored ritual, after all; no one would suspect she was malingering.

As to the Buddha, there comes a time for conventional imagery. There is a moment when one must chose the prayer mat or beads, some recognizable affiliation to get mail from in the holiday season, to bake cookies and breads for, to send the children. Why not him, Buddha, with his fat belly and face that looks as if he has just unified the theory of the fields. He has solved the ultimate equation and decided to tell no one, to burn his notebooks, to watch them float like parched lilies over the rocks and further, into the current that leads to the sea.

She is winding up and down aisles of Buddhas, surveying the types, wood and tin and stone, carved and painted and glazed. Now he is serious. Now he is decadent, leaning back after eating or drinking too much, bloated, holding what might be a ledger.

She has been searching for a Buddha since college, but she never finds the right one. How is she to know? She touches the carved wood and stone, the bronze, plastic, and jade. Nothing stings or burns. There is no caress, no sense of resolution. He is fattened with arrogance, he looks like a pedophile, and suddenly she doesn't want him.

There will be no way to select a tea set, either. How could she choose between the cherry blossoms, the fish, the horse heads, the branches holding what appear to be severed hearts? Then one with a man grasping what might be a scroll or a sword. Which should a woman drink from? Where does knowledge lie? Are they Buddhas or warriors or some phase in transition, a man's depiction of the evolution of personality that doesn't interest her? She touches a Buddha in a material that mimics gold, is instead a kind of tin that could cut the fingers. You could kiss him and your mouth would fill with blood.

She feels a form of corruption is coming directly from these statues. It's a low-grade pollution with a cumulative effect. It begins as a sickness in the tiny hot rooms without windows where such souvenir items are contrived in Pacific Rim cities on streets of mud ruts and broken stones. The tarnished objects are unloaded by men in docks and harbors where Asian women with red lipstick and unzipped blue jeans smile their many lies that do not require translation.

In the harbors and ports, men imagine taking these women home. In the backs of their bedrooms are altars made from old tiles and strips of wood. An engorged Buddha with a painted green robe has American dollar bills stuffed under each fat arm. He smiles behind candles in tin holders. A dish with rancid oranges is placed in front of the platform, as if he were a dog. In the corner of the platform, in a jar that once contained food, there is sand, three peacock feathers, and slim sticks of incense with names corresponding to psychological and physical conditions, to harbors and rivers, spices and flowers.

Caroline picks up a teacup and turns it in her hand. It is entirely enameled, it seems flowered and burning, hot and alive. Could a woman really drink from this? It occurs to her that such patterns confuse the wind, make it lose direction and smell different. Something happens with the spices, the harvest and currents. It induces a minute adjustment in the aesthetic, just enough to provide a small startlement, a moment when a woman can't breathe.

Such a rearrangement could chance to learn the art of rebirthing itself, and then you wouldn't recognize anything. This is the process by which people change and disappear. There are degrees of variation. Sometimes one returns from lunch and merely requires a nap or a divorce. The alteration can be more dramatic. That is when they never find the body, not even after they've dispatched a dozen boats, dragged the harbor from side to side, even sent men with oxygen strapped to their backs off the edges of slow barges.

She leans against a brick building near a newsstand. A woman with lips lined with lacquers that seem to have fallen from sunset skies in a series of scented reds and transmuted magical bloods takes up three-quarters of the front page. She looks as if she is saying, this is why you must kiss.

Caroline considers the implications. There are no simple lines between acts of fraudulence and enchantment, between what is called tarnished and what is bewitched. It is a continuum, and at the end the saints bleed roses from their punctures. You could walk through the valley of the beheaded and assemble flower arrangements that would last forever. All the women serving sweet-and-sour pork and chicken curry in the Thai restaurants of Hollywood know this. And the Vietnamese sisters who open nail-polishing salons in Santa Monica, who are the keepers of the pinks, the secrets of sculpted extensions and China silk wraps know this feminine calligraphy.

Always, the women return with their painted nails and raise them to their faces and farther. They have torches at the tips of their fingers. There are moments of flame. They know then that they are lighthouses, the method by which the men calculate where and how to return.

Caroline becomes aware of a blond man climbing the hill below her. She has been watching him taking his measured steps. She thinks this blond man with long hair looks like a photographer. He wears his hair long because he made certain vows in the '60s and he honors them. They share certain principles.

In his studio, she would find Hendrix and Traffic tapes. They could talk about the Fillmore Auditorium. When she had two dollars and fifty cents she would hitchhike into the City, watch the Jefferson Airplane perform, the Quicksilver Messenger Service, the Grateful Dead, and once, on New Year's Eve, the Who. They played all night.

It was raining. She danced with herself under strobe lights.

She could ask the blond man if he remembers her, with her long red skirt in the corner, barefoot on the floor that was a sequence of galaxies rising and falling. She could ask him questions about various types of teas and their nuances. Then she could go home with him.

He could take black-and-white photographs of her naked with the harbor at her back. Her breasts would merge with the domes of buildings. Her thoughts would be shadows and patches of sudden fierce sunlight. It would look as if spires were growing from her spine. She would be a kind of land mass where everything was inert, and she would be the most quiet of all the shapes. She would be the core, the place with the ancient smooth stones where all the ships come to anchor. The rows of houses on the hills behind her would be ridges of scales, and she would be the dragon lady. At last she would know exactly what to do. She would open her mouth and breathe fire.

The man wears a beige raincoat, carries an umbrella, and passes without glancing at her. It occurs to Caroline that she could walk down any of the network of branching alleys off the narrow streets and a whole other life would begin.

She could not count the lives she has entered and shed, apartments rented and abandoned, houses, clothing left in closets, tubers planted in rainstorms she didn't see come up, the pinyon and red juniper cut but never burned. The plans for the fence, the pool, the garden waterfall, all the outlines with ink and numbers left rolled up on thin sheets of paper somewhere. Such pages do not fade. They remain as surely as ports on maps. These are the passages where one docked, spent a weekend or a year.

It is one-fifteen and there are banners across the crowded streets and she is beginning to decipher Chinese. The script repeats phrases from the cracked open bellies of fortune cookies. Beauty, prosperity, health, peace, dreamless nights, obedient children, decades of rice harvest, a bridge across a river people must cross and you can stand under a straw umbrella taxing them. Of course the scroll-like banners across the streets must be advertising these possibilities, but which ones does a woman need most? Can you collect several? Is there a hierarchy, a limit, and who decides?

She finds herself entering a shop displaying herbs that resemble dried reptiles. There are shelves of tentacled whitish things that look cramped and alive and clearly planning another ocean crossing. Should a woman come at night and release them? Of course these herbs will do anything, but what is it she wants done? She must be specific. Telepathy cannot be liquid. She knows this. There are answers, but she must frame the questions and the parameters. She learned this at the university.

She has reached the bottom of the hill; she can see the gate. This will be the last corner with young Asian women smiling through their tainted mouths on the covers of magazines. The shops have become generic and marginal, haphazard with pennants for a variety of cities and sporting teams and shirts with caricatures of cable cars and bridges stenciled on them. Now there are stores with radios and little boxes you give to children and over-sized pencils and tablecloths with embroidered edges.

Caroline will never master the intricacies of cloisonné, not the flowers and birds on vases and serving dishes and the sides of pens and the holders for daggers. She will never comprehend the legends associated with owls and snails, frogs and bells or the cloisonné horses that might be paperweights. She will not purchase a tea set with elephants along the rim or trays with herons or cranes. There is a history to these pigs and eggs, but she recognizes that for her it is too late.

American and Chinese disco music plays tinny on the tables where radios and tape decks and video machines are sold. Neil Diamond sings "Kentucky Woman" over and over. The quality of the music feels cheap. It makes the air spoiled. It soils it.

It is downhill now, past a shop where swans have been constructed from pearls. There are pearl goats, and temples carved out of what appears to be ivory. She notices a vase near the doorway, a vase so tall she could hide in it. Maybe that's the ticket, she thinks. Crawling back into a womb that could really protect you this time. Something coldly enameled, metallic, covered with savage birds. And bells are striking the half hour. There is a church behind brick courtyard walls. Then she has left Chinatown.

When Evan pointed to their hotel from the taxi, she had seen the two flags at the top. Just look for the flags, Evan reminded her. But now, as she approaches the downtown nest of spires, there are flags on all the roofs.

She asks a man in a dark blue business suit for directions. "Excuse me," Caroline begins, but he has backed away, sidestepped her. He walks faster and doesn't turn back.

She attempts to get directions from two other men. They do not look at her, and one crosses to the other side of the street. Caroline is thirty-eight years old and her hair is almost down to her waist, windblown, it might be a sort of curling black fishing net with a baseball cap bobbing on the top. She is wearing army surplus fatigue pants, cowboy boots, and a black leather jacket Evan bought her in London. Perhaps she doesn't look right, she decides, clearly alien to this sequence of skyscrapers all with flags on their roofs.

Then she remembers it is San Francisco, a port city in a plague year, and no one permits strangers to approach them. Anyone might suddenly succumb to a spasm, reach out, bite the flesh of a pedestrian, and there would be a terrible prolonged death. There would be stigma and gossip.

Perhaps women with hair like nets for catching fish are suspect. Women are considered dangerous in port cities where the ships could be bringing in anything. It's always that way, diseases that don't even have names yet, carried along with the cargoes of rancid fruit that spoil the air, liquids that spill from carcasses in the holds and make the gulls die, make the crab and bass go away. In port cities there is always a traffic in rumor. This is what Caroline is thinking as she asks six people which way her hotel is. Finally a woman tells her where to turn.

In the lobby Caroline stuffs her jacket pockets with nuts from the bowls on the bar. She forces herself to eat them in the elevator. She doesn't want Evan to think she hasn't been taking care of herself. It is essential that she not appear dizzy or faltering, in some way out of focus and not herself. She might become suspect. A woman who could begin wailing from gutters with her black pearl hair in the slow sun, obviously inhuman, the fibers on her back collecting tiny flecks and orbs that might be edible, might be useful. Men with guns would have to take such a woman away.

Caroline closes the door to the hotel room where she fell in love. It occurs to her that there is a certain horror to rooms visited periodically. They are just familiar enough to induce a persistent form of disorientation. It is in such rooms that one loses not one's leather jacket and silver bracelets but pieces of the self. They are left on the sheets, in the bathtub, on the silk floral seat beside the window. This is the sort of debris that attracts fog and feeds storms.

Caroline has returned to the room first. It is essential that she position herself correctly. San Francisco spreads itself below, opening its avenues of inflammation, taunting one to kiss here above the harbor and the lamps. The sky and bay are an identical uninterrupted blue that makes her think, simultaneously, of trespass and grace.

It is her fifth anniversary. Now she hears the turning of the doorknob. She rises, rushes to the window, placing herself between him and the city. There can be no other trajectory, no other point of entry. He cannot see the bridges or the bay or the channel that runs beneath the

Golden Gate to China without first noticing her face. There is an intricate choreography of sailboats in the harbor, ferries and ships carrying rumors and corrupted cargo, but he will see her eyes and mouth first.

She is intrinsic to this landscape, this portscape. She might be something the sea washed in. She is his version of the women with the names of flowers lacquered to their fingertips. Her lips are a delicacy of fragrant reds like the women on magazine covers on corner newsstands above harbors, beside channels and inlets and the gulfs between islands. Women of palms and rivers. Women with fishing nets on their backs.

Evan is smiling, walking toward her. He understands that the spires of the city are growing out of her spine. He sees that the ridges of hillside houses are scales across her back. He recognizes that she is the dragon lady. He is certain her fire is for him and him only. He knows this because she is poised above the bay and she is on time.

Caroline is thinking the women stand at windows with the golden bands of their wedding rings glowing on their fingers like beacons in lighthouses. They have stopped traveling, and these are their luminescent conspiracies. This is why the men go and how they return. It is always a plague year, abrupt and treacherous. And it is the dragon ladies and fire women, in silent conjunction, who open their arms to form the contours of the world.

something particular about the nature of midnight

It is New Year's Eve, 1981. Rachel Stein prepares to remember this night, to map and preserve it in a kind of invisible neural acid. Such a process must be possible. This night is a psychic embryo. It will enter the fibers of her flesh and mate with her cells. It will settle in, and she will have this film as long as she breathes. This is the substance she really required all along, something tougher than the photographs she once thought she needed. They were the fraudulence. This, on the other hand, is more deceptive and permanent.

Rachel Stein is alone with her infant who she must soon name. It's been three weeks since she took the baby home from the hospital in a taxicab. Her parents didn't come to the hospital. They have decided this event has not occurred. They have no vocabulary to define it so they have deleted it from their consciousness. She thinks it is curious, how they could drive her to airports where planes would take her to countries wracked by civil wars, regions with plagues and no roads and teenagers in the trees with automatic weapons. But they could not admit to this configuration, their daughter with the infant and no husband.

It was raining when she took her infant home in the cab. There were rules that were bent for her. She still had certain connections. She still knew how to evoke names, how to toss them into conversations like hand grenades. She wasn't like the other unwed mothers. Her mother was a psychologist. The other unwed mothers had mothers who worked as domestics.

From her wheelchair in the rain at the curb of the hospital, holding the infant that did not seem natural or part of her—seemed like a generic product that had been handed to her, shoes, perhaps, or eight pounds of books—she decided to reassess her perception of the other unwed mothers. At least their families arrived to escort them home. Rachel watched their departures from the lobby, how siblings offered garish oversized balloons, there were boxes of chocolates, there were grandmothers with shawls and no English and laughter.

Rachel had told her doctor that she needed to live with her daughter first. She could not simply assign a name to this small and utterly alien thing that she had somehow and inexplicably been given. What Rachel meant was that she thought this baby would communicate with her. By some mysterious process, it would let its preferences be known. It. The baby.

Now it is three weeks since that day and the baby still has no name. It has blond hair and a weak mouth that does not retain its shape. It is a hole, a black tunnel in the face, and it doesn't seem possible that it belongs to her. It is raining incredibly hard, unusually hard. There are streaks of lightning and the almost immediate crash of thunder. There are sudden small yellow explosions on the periphery. She imagines it as a kind of perimeter strung with barbed wire. But she doesn't bother to get up from the sofa, carry her daughter in her arms, walk to the window, look out.

Rachel doesn't even glance at the rain because she no longer believes there can be revelations through climate. There was a part of her once that would, in a micro-second, amass, assemble, collate, and arrange into chronological order all the phenomena she had experienced. It never occurred to her that these events were not a form of knowledge that would provide clarity and solace. She had thought it simply a matter of time. She would decipher it, find the right angle, the source of light, where the background should be.

She viewed her life as a photographic sequence of striking and disturbing elements. She was there to snap the shot and provide a simple text. The autumn a hurricane hit the tip of Kauai, she stayed until there were no planes out. The series of gray waves were thirty feet high, small cities with steeples and cathedrals breaking below the cliffs where she stood in a wind seemingly alone. But she was there with her camera, looking them in the eye. It was the history of architecture she saw breaking at her feet.

She enjoyed dealing in fluid devastation. She considered the flood in Sonoma. They said the highway was closed, and she ignored them, displayed her press card, drove to the place where the road had been and was now erased. At that edge, she watched bits of a bridge drift toward the sea, dragging its metal and cables behind it, then the pieces of houses, two golden retrievers on what had once been a second-story terrace. She took out her camera. An entire house dropped into the river. She watched it return to its basic elements, redwood into water, glass into sand, all of it being drawn to the ocean, and it was as it should be.

Rachel had been diligent with her observations. She had courted the brutally intense. She cannot count the times she had deliberately gotten sunburned or wet, bitten by insects, been uncomfortable, caught a cold or an infection for the sake of a certain slope of cloud.

There had been the electrical storms she had seen from a houseboat on Lake Powell in Utah or Arizona, the way they continued for days without a map through plazas of mesa, everything too vivid, too overly clarified. The world was opened surgically. It was misshapen, anatomical, the rocks reminded her of the striations in muscle. She had finally gotten in and the earth was an autopsy. She shot sixty rolls.

In the afternoon she swam from the boat, and the current was sudden and fierce. She felt a gulf open beneath her feet, pulling her toes. It was green, the essence of all elements unleashed and untamed, and it seemed somehow musical. It contained the quality of certain strange songs, like the sequence of howls coyotes make, and she wanted to listen. There were fluid epics, she was certain. And the man she had been with that week, the man who had managed to lose the map, said he was certain she was going to drown.

Later that summer she had been rained on in the Snake River in a raft. It was some assignment about vestiges of the real West or the Old West. She had eaten spoiled chili the night before. Then wind was blowing in her face, and she saw only the red baseball cap she was wearing. There was the sense of damp bitter weeds. Everything was misted and broken, and she still took photographs. When her hand shook, she bit it. She had discovered that pain was anchoring. Sometimes it was the only way to get the job done.

There are the rains we invent, she thinks, holding the baby that looks nothing like her, the undefined infant she is supposed to name. There are the rains when we take the ordinary and minor observation and arrange the details to provide the appearance of the definitive. There is no fraud in that. It's a kind of art. Rachel had often taken unremarkable afternoons and forced them to their edge, prying off their secret skins, leaving them naked and shuddering.

She did that in Seattle, from her hotel window in an almost- autumn, shooting out across the bay and smoking marijuana. The invented rains, she thinks. Then there are the rains that find us when we are not looking, when we are quiet and ask for nothing. Or perhaps these are the rains that actually invent us. And none of it mattered, Rachel concludes. None of it made her more intelligent, competent, or secure. None of it gave her the names for a baby.

In fact, Rachel Stein is beginning to doubt all the intrinsic impulses that fed her across the years, the foundations and perimeters. The idea that there is fluid revelation, that in waters wisdom accrues and can be distilled, translated, known, passed on. If you can find the one moment when light and shadow open into absolute destiny, then you can snap this in a photograph and decode the meaning of the world. You can know her camouflaged seconds, infiltrate and imprison them. You can outwit time. You can make your own fossils. You are the keeper of the amber. You can trap creatures in this, and they will be perfect in five hundred million years. In between, you can tape them to walls, mount them like the heads of animals. You can hang them in galleries. It is time itself that you are looking at. And you can hunt these images in your own season with your heart aching as you feel the world become too small, old, stripped.

Now Rachel Stein is beginning to distrust the entire subterranean strata that formed the basis of her life. That is why she ignores the rain. It's the first rain in months in what is obviously the relentless drought condition of Southern California. It is not an aberration but the natural climate. Why don't they simply admit this instead of announcing each year as a new drought. Now it may not rain again for decades, and she doesn't care.

In truth, rain never cleansed her, it never purified anything. There was no clarification through water. As to the photographs yanked from the debris, you could look at them mounted in a frame like a mirror, but they didn't speak. Rachel thinks it absurd that she could have ever thought this was a possibility. Of course, no intelligence forms in any fluid, not even vodka. The fact that she could have seriously considered this means she must distrust other fundamental concepts about herself. Then how will she ever name this infant? And if she doesn't return the official name form tomorrow, will they take the baby away? Will she be charged with some sort of baby abuse? Will her friends know?

Rachel considers the implications, and it's not just the rain. She's noticed she doesn't take the seat next to the window on airplanes anymore. This happened even before she was pregnant. She didn't ask before checking in if her room in the hotel faced the ocean, the forest, the mountains or lake. She doesn't reach for her camera anymore when the pilot says they are above yet another river, another desert, they are passing over a certain monument, a trade route, a gulf. It has recently occurred to her that all the ocean and desert and forest views she has accumulated, privately stalked and captured, have failed her. The canyon crossings, the arroyos with their suggestion of bobcats and owls and something green howling in an impenetrable night, are false, provide no answers, no fire, no illumination, no inscription to tell her the name of her child.

The last time she was in London, Rachel declined an afternoon in the British Museum. She has never seen the domed room where Virgina Woolf wrote, and she has become glad of this. Always before, on the day she was there, it was being restored or the season or the hour was wrong. Now Rachel wants to make certain she never sees it. She wasn't pregnant yet when she refused to walk along the Thames, went back to her hotel alone instead, ordered a bottle of vodka, drew a line of cocaine. She put her camera on the television set, zipped it shut in the case, thinking that she could not accommodate another river or museum, another set of Egyptian princes and kings, more corridors of looted goods.

Rachel had once been convinced there was an irrefutable sincerity in sand and rock that long-dead men had arranged with their fingers. Now it is of little interest. What did she learn from architecture? What did she learn from walking along beaches, watching one impaled sun or another splinter and spray its debris across clouds, rendering them the orange of translucent abuse, wounded and ecstatic with pain.

Of course, all skies are archetypal and say the same thing. They have no intrinsic meaning. It is only what the observer decides, what the photographer manages to imply. How many times did she have to learn this?

Her infant cries, and she puts the baby against her breast. It slowly drinks her milk. This process is more horrible than boring, and there is nothing natural about it. The blond baby will never be mistaken for hers. People in supermarkets and airports will think she is an aunt or a friend. The baby is strange and ugly. She cannot imagine always having it with her. She cannot even bring herself to name it. How can she possess this thing?

It occurs to her that the big occasions and great events have left her stranded and empty. Bodies and bridges fallen, burned, drowned. The crash of forty-foot waves, and if it isn't the snapping of photographs, if it isn't the click, click of I have you, you're mine forever, then what can it possibly be?

For instance, her grandmother is dying in a sort of slow motion. If anyone wanted to say goodbye, even as a petty aside, a sort of veiled afterthought, there is time. Her grandmother has had a series of heart attacks, and in between she is hospitalized for months, entire seasons. She watches the trees change in the parking lot below. One could pick a season, orchestrate a spring or fall farewell.

Rachel often thought of her grandmother's impending death. She was waiting for a sign, some indication of when she should call. Rachel was the oldest grandchild, the firstborn. She waited until her daughter was born. It was December.

She walked through her house with the infant in its special crocheted blanket. She circled her house, room to room, for hours. She was afraid to put the baby down. Then she called her grandmother in a hospital named for a marginal president in a section of New York City where she had never been, had seen from the highway, had not even bothered to photograph. Rachel had thought this birth combined with the impending death was a rare confluence in which wisdom should be transmitted.

Rachel Stein had taken her grandmother's hospital phone number months before. It was taped to her refrigerator where it seemed that the most important external elements of her life were kept, the numbers on her medical insurance cards, the telephone number of the pediatrician, the taxi company and liquor store that delivered until midnight. Rachel had to telephone the hospital numerous times. After all, she did not really know her grandmother. There had always been a continent between them. In her family there was perpetual turmoil, small crude wars and exiles within exile. There were inexplicable absences and raw places that could not be spoken of or touched. Names were banished, histories denied and canceled. There was the sense that as you stood there, some bridge was being dynamited. There was smoke in your face and the constant sensation of falling.

"Are you afraid of dying?" Rachel finally asked the grandmother she barely knew.

She had only one old photograph of her grandmother, a black-and-white where she was an infant sitting on her grandmother's lap. She seemed a reasonable woman in a flowered print dress, a plump woman with long hair in a bun and a weary smile. What could her grandmother have done to deserve her exile, the years when she was never mentioned? Her mother had no mother. That was what her family said. Her mother often claimed that she was actually an orphan. Her mother was fond of saying that she had given birth to herself.

"Of course, I'm afraid," her grandmother said. Her words were heavily accented. She was smoking. The voice was hoarse.

There did not seem to be any sequence of responses that were appropriate. After awhile, Rachel said, "It's okay. It's human to be afraid."

"Do I care if it's allowed or not?" her grandmother demanded. "I'm afraid," she repeated. "I'm afraid."

That was their first conversation on the first afternoon when she brought her unnamed daughter home. Rachel has read a statistic that the majority of terminal patients live to their next birthday and die shortly after. Her grandmother's birthday is in May. Rachel expects her to live until spring.

Rachel had wanted to tell her grandmother that she had given birth to a daughter. This would be her grandmother's first great- grandchild. But Rachel stopped herself. She realized there was something horrible in it. Her grandmother was dying in a welfare hospital, alone in winter. Her daughter did not recognize her life or impending death. Her daughter called herself an orphan. This same grandmother had given birth in another New York City hospital without a husband. Now Rachel had borne a daughter, also in winter, also without a husband. Her mother did not speak to either of them. They had both been penalized. Of course, their circumstances were different, the intricacies, the motivation and sociology. Or were they?

Now there would be one more of them and one less. And Rachel recognized that this was another one of the big occasions that would fail her. Its promise of ineluctable clarity would remain unfulfilled, stunted, veiled. It would become the color of winter silence, which is a strained pale like a bruise that has already partially healed. You wear it but you can't remember why. It's the color of hallucination.

Rachel rocked her baby. She carried the phone to the sofa. She realized that this was an emotional configuration that would remain locked. It was little different than a city, flying over or landing in it, touring it by car or jeep or limousine. And if it wasn't a city, if it wasn't a forest or beach, a desert or jungle, if it wasn't Thanksgiving or Passover or Memorial Day, if it wasn't birth or death, what the hell was it? How did you find it? When you got there, how would you know? Should you take a camera? Should you take an automatic weapon, canned goods, lamps? Would you need boxes of trinkets for the natives, red beads that glittered, square pocket mirrors and objects in brass?

Rachel had been searching for something definitive since her first photograph. She had not found it. Certainly it wasn't graduating from the university. It wasn't the marriages or divorces. It wasn't the one-woman show in Los Angeles or New York. It wasn't the first or second grant or fellowship. It wasn't Bombay at sundown or Paris at night. Now there was her grandmother's slow arabesque down. Now there was the sound of her infant daughter wailing, inhuman, in the winter night.

Rachel slowly began to think of her grandmother by name, Pearl. She found she could telephone her grandmother Pearl when she woke up to feed and change her baby at two and four o'clock, alone, in the California December. It was dawn then in New York. Pearl was waiting for her. She never thought to ask why this granddaughter was awake so early or so often.

Rachel would hold her daughter to her breast and dial Pearl. It was dawn and still snowing in New York. Rachel was aware that there was a complete circle of women alone in rooms in winter. Her brand-new baby, who seemed to resist a name, who did not yet inhabit any of the syllables she had temporarily contrived for her. Then her dying grandmother on the other coast, more syllables without substance. These were elements of winter, sounds with the intention of becoming something, but they were not yet formed. Winter sounds were embryonic. They were condensed designs that could become anything. Rachel would hold her daughter and talk to her grandmother Pearl. She thought this should be a circle that could speak, but she sensed it would not.

"I dreamed John Kennedy was making love to me," Pearl said. "He was coming for me on a boat. He looked exactly like I remember, with the fancy overcoat on, smiling. Remember the teeth? The smile? He was reaching out to me. He was carrying flowers."

It would be early morning in New York. Snow was falling. Rachel tried to imagine this other coast. She considers the way certain overcast evenings in the mountains are, when everything is silver and pine needles look stenciled against the slate air. They remind her of a process she suddenly remembers from first or second grade, perhaps something where one blows on ink and makes snowflakes.

In Southern California it is 3 A.M. She feels unfocused and bruised. She wonders if this is the beginning of what they call blue. If this were true, it might get colder. There could be unspeakable internal rearrangements. Then she telephones her grandmother. Rachel wants to tell her that she has been abandoned by her parents. She resists.

"I dreamed the building was on fire," Pearl says. She's been waiting for her granddaughter to call. "I break a window with my shoe. I'm young. I have high heels. No arthritis. I'm wearing silver lamé with fox on the cuffs. I never had a get-up like that, believe me. Not once in my life. I look like Bette Davis. I break the window and I don't get cut. I look out. On a ladder, a fireman is coming to save me. Then I see. He's holding a hose in one hand and flowers in the other. I see the flowers so clearly. They're so big. There's nothing wrong with my eyes. I don't even have glasses. Orchids and gardenias. That's what he's carrying. You know what that would cost? And you know who is coming?"

"Who?" Rachel asks.

"It's John Kennedy," Pearl says.

It occurs to Rachel that there is a sort of quiet only a woman alone with a crying baby can know. Or a woman caught between seizures of the heart. We are all living between seizures of the heart, Rachel decides as her baby nurses and her grandmother reveals that she has again dreamed of water or fire, boats and ladders, flames and ocean, wood and flowers. This is her grandmother's alphabet at the end, recurrent and boldly inflamed. These are Pearl's final photographs.

"It's like going to the movies," Pearl said. "I never knew so much was in my head. So many characters. So many colors. I might have done things different."

"What would you have done differently?" she asks.

Rachel wants to know. She closes her eyes. She is prepared for enormities. She will open her mouth and receive the communion she has always and secretly longed for. She is prepared to speak in tongues and know God. She is willing to throw her cane away and walk. She is ready for the show in the tent. She is thirty-two years old and alone with an infant who has no name, and it is raining.

"Who knows? Maybe something with pictures. Something with paints." Her grandmother sounds on the verge of tears. "Are you the one with all the pictures? The pictures in magazines?"

"Yes," Rachel says. "What else would you do over?"

Pearl is thinking. Rachel can hear her expel smoke. "I might have opened a flower shop," she says. "I could have got the money." Then she begins crying.

Rachel hangs up the telephone. Her infant is crying. Her grandmother is crying. Two out of three is enough. There is a perfect circle of women alone in winter with their names insubstantial, women with experiences that should be engraved in flame or stone but are not. Their lives will be less than footnotes. And if it isn't the click, if it isn't in the frame, if it isn't waiting in the shadow or sunlight, what is it? Not this incoherent circle that might as well be mute.

It is at moments like this, at junctures that only appear after midnight, when Rachel Stein considers the possibility that she has somehow fallen off the girders, out of the plot. She was always the careful girl, the one who got straight A's, who never broke a bone. The girl who won the talent show. You didn't need to tell her to practice piano, to check her math twice. She was the one with the best summer adventure, the first girl with bangs, white lipstick, and jazz albums. How was she removed from the standard story, which wrong path did she take? What could possibly have crawled in from the edge, what whispered in her ear, what incantation led her to be sent home in a taxicab in a rain storm, alone with an infant?

She was always looking for the singular. She admits this. If it wasn't a city or a way of touring it, of learning the language and monuments, if it wasn't a region or season or landscape, perhaps it was a chemical, something you could ingest. That was when she had started her internal experiments, went to the Yucatán to eat peyote, claimed she was photographing pyramids. Later, she smoked hash along the banks of the Ganges. It was about taking better photographs. It was about nuance and shadow. It was about learning how to look into rivers like they were mirrors of time, portals that dreamed in blue. Then one day she stopped asking for the window seat. It was better away from the river with its predictable rancid debris. She preferred spending the evening alone with a bottle in her hotel room.

Rachel Stein walks with her baby in nervous circles. The baby looks nothing like her. Her life has been a catalog of failed gestures, some of them matted, framed, published. There was always the sudden inspiration of rebellion and how it soured. All dawns became similar, bands of estranged grays. Eventually she will take her baby into bed with her. They will hear the wind. She will think, there is wind and the absolute failure of everything but breath.

But now, walking in a sequence of circles—she is afraid to count their number—Rachel feels as if everything is swaying. The continent is swaying. It is inhabited by women rocking their infants to sleep. Rachel is part of an enormous midnight circle of women alone in winter. It is a time when everything is silvered and stalled. It is here women build their silent architectures with gestures that cannot be measured or repeated. They are too spontaneous and complicated. They lack the framework of intention.

The women are walking through the perimeters of their rooms, rocking infants and talking the almost-dead to sleep with their loom voices. It is a world of gray congruencies, ruled by the repetition of circumstance. There are shadows and duplications that insinuate themselves into the future.

Rachel imagines all the women waiting in midnight, standing on piers they have somehow arrived at. Many are uncertain of where they are or why. The light is oddly amber and warm. It is old light. It contains lost properties of how to assemble objects for auguries, of how to clear the lungs. A boat is coming to save you. You are absolutely certain. A great man will offer you a bouquet of silver roses, violet orchids, gardenias out of season. Here there are no shadows, only the arc cast by complexities the color of sails, rain-driven. Everything is amber and manila like canvas seen by lamps in fog.

Rachel stands at the window with her infant. She must name her. There are places where the wood sill is imperfect and the draft rushes in. The air smells singed. It must have something to do with the thunder and the fireworks, the way someone on the next street is shooting a gun. Is it possible there is sulfur between the citrus and the jasmine? Somehow, the earth has been turned.

Rachel lies in bed with her infant. She expects her grandmother to telephone, to wish her a happy New Year, but she doesn't. Her grandmother will not telephone again. Pearl is dead. She died before midnight. The statistics were wrong. A nurse will find her phone number on Pearl's bedside table and telephone her early in the morning. That will be her first call on the first day of the new year.

Rachel has come to understand something about the

nature of midnight. She imagines all the silent women sorting buttons in their sewing boxes by lamplight. Can anyone believe they are really arranging them by color, that the shape of these buttons are somehow arousing their interest? When the women are looking at linens, holding them in their fingers, is it possible they are really calculating their fray?

Someday a man will ask, while she kneels in a hallway picking up towels, surveying them by wear, what are you thinking? Rachel knows this will happen. And she will answer, *nothing*.

Or perhaps it will occur in an elegant Italian restaurant, festive, with miniature pink flowers in a good crystal vase. He will say, what are you thinking? And she will say, *just something about midnight in winter.*

When the women seem to be exploring avenues of color at the lipstick counter, they are really considering some other spectrum entirely. It is always a night like this that they are remembering. It lacked a vocabulary even as it was happening. There were fantastic constructions. The night was etched. It had substance like metal or clay, you could pound and sculpt it. There were avenues and bridges, and then they were suddenly gone. This is what the women are thinking.

And the last sound Rachel hears might be thunder or firecrackers or gunshots. It is midnight precisely. She can hear cars honking their horns through the rain. She is holding her daughter in her arms and she thinks, suddenly, that she will name her Pearl.

Outside, on a nearby hill, boys are setting off fireworks between the weeds and concrete and mud. Sparklers are tattooing the dark with electric swirls. The remnants of larger burnt configurations resembling brutal flowers are dissolving to the wet earth. They fall, leaving slow trails like dissected stars or molecules with their structures exposed, blazing conceptual skeletons.

Rachel closes her eyes and feels her bed is rocking, the

entire region is rocking, it is always rocking. And somewhere men on wooden ships are bringing bouquets of rare and luminous roses the color of burning fireworks to all the women who are there, who have always been there, in the amber shadows, waiting.

histories of the undead

When Erica took a leave of absence to complete her research she knew almost immediately that she would fail. She devised lists of people to telephone, penciled in a schedule of interviews and columns with questions. Her handwriting seemed small and bruised. She called no one.

She remembers now, in the long mornings when Flora and Bob are gone, that she always detested fragments. Or more accurately, the need to order them, to invent a spine, a progression, a curve that resolves.

She is, at her core, too nervous, restless, and cynical. There is something within her that can only say no. It's odd that she thought she had subdued this, found her own rain forest, slashed and burned it to the last acre of cold ash. She wonders if she should be grateful. Perhaps somewhere on a balcony, in a permanently ochre-tinted city she isn't certain of, there is more air for someone, a woman standing mute and confused in a scented dusk, a woman searching for something.

It was late morning. Day was elbowing clouds above glazed roofs of orange tiles, and she feels startled and amazed. Seen from the right angle, the city is a sequence of seashells, glistening abalone, their bellies an offering of mother-of-pearl. She became aware of the fact that she wasn't worried about abandoning her project or the implications this might have on her tenure profile. She had always sensed a rainy day coming. It would be an afternoon in winter when some massive typhoon would speak her name. There would be a new fluid language, a kind of cursive rendered in acid. Then it would invade her lungs, she would be singed, and it would be the time of the drowning.

It occurred to her that the suddenness with which her behavior altered had a predestined quality. It was as if she had been secretly engaged in a dress rehearsal for precisely this abandonment and divestiture all of her life. This knowledge entered her with a fierce urgency. It felt perpetual and alluring, like sin or revelation. It was inescapable. She recognized it as a kind of return. It had always been there. This was the cove where she was meant to anchor.

This must be what she was thinking about at traffic lights, why she didn't play her car radio and was never bored, why the static in the air seemed a kind of hieroglyphic she tried to decipher. This must be why she would walk out of theaters and not remember the title of the play, the setting, or even the genre. Had it been a musical, a love story, or a comedy? She would walk across a parking lot shaking her head.

Perhaps she had been tuned into another station entirely. There was something on the margin that attracted her, something in the extreme edge of the register where you couldn't be certain of dates or motives or outcome. She could never understand, really, why the motion picture was more interesting than sitting in the lobby with the carpet that looked like stained glass in reverse, deco blood petals, panels of crimson and lime that marked not translucency but rather the end of the line. Here couples glared at each other above the too-yellow popcorn and all things were random, vaguely metallic and swollen. She thought of hooks that were swallowed. And why was this less significant than the other images, the ones you sat in dark rooms for, sat as if a subliminal force were fattening you for a harvest or a kill.

Erica realized that time would pass and her grant would expire. The questions she had planned to examine seemed distant and trivial. She wondered if it were possible to be defined by refusal. Certainly the most brilliant of her subjects would listen to her questions, run a slow hand across a soft mouth, and remain silent. She was looking out the kitchen window when she realized this. There were five pigeons on a strip of grass, and the red bands around their necks were exactly the same shade of corrupted pink as the red *no stopping* lines painted on the curb in front of their house. Had she finally discovered something?

She began to sleep past eight o'clock. She could not drive her daughter to school. She was no longer reliable. Now she called a taxicab for her daughter the night before, gave Flora ten dollars, told her to wait outside, and to keep the change. She reminded Flora not to mention this to Bob. She squeezed Flora's shoulder with her fingers when she said this.

When Erica woke up late she made a second pot of coffee, put brandy in it, ate an extra piece of toast, layered it with jam. She turned on the stereo. The concept of rock and roll in the morning by sunlight was stunning.

Her husband came home for lunch. She hadn't expected him. She was looking out the kitchen window. There was a tarnish in the air, a sort of glaze.

Perhaps it was part of a complicated cleaning solution with invisible ammonia. It was designed to bring out the shine, but the sky was overcast.

"You seem troubled," Bob said. He put his briefcase on the table. Its proportion seemed monumental. "Is it the research?"

She shook her head, no. It was nearly noon. It was the hour the workingmen sat on lawns smoking cigarettes and eating lunches that looked too meager to sustain them.

They leaned close to one another, planning burglaries and trading lies about women.

"You aren't yourself," Bob decided. He paused and studied her face. "I don't have to go to Seattle. Christ. I don't even have a paper to present."

Erica said, "Don't be silly. I'm perfectly fine."

Later, she stood in the backyard where the bushes were trimmed and resembled elongated skulls. She had forgotten he was going to a conference. Now that she knew he would be gone this night and the next, she wondered if his absence mattered. Was it fundamental, was it definitive, would there be change? She leaned against the side of the house. These were the stark fragments that bruised, made you fall, made you hoarse. It was best to create methods of walking with your eyes shut.

Bob noticed that she was different but his conclusion was wrong. He could observe but not interpret. She was merely in transition. She was returning to a version of a former self. And Erica wondered how she would devise a process of clarification, how she would problem-solve this small confusion of who she was.

Whenever she encountered enormities, Erica could only think of walking beside water, a bay or a rocky stretch of coast, or finding her daughter, holding Flora and breathing in the scent of her black hair, which was the spiced essence of night rivers. They were the only two manifestations in the landscape that were indisputable, like a certain sequence of spires, of bridges or plazas. This was how she could know where she was. Geography would form a rudimentary net, the first in a series of coordinates. Later she could build a landing strip.

Erica walks into the early afternoon, uncertain of where she is going. There is only a sense of fluid depth and the realization that she is again thinking about her sister Ellen. Her sister has two best friends and both of them are dying. These two other women, barely nodding acquaintances, have somehow achieved a massive presence in Erica's life. Often her sister will telephone with frantic updates on the brutal unravelings of the other women. It is curious how Lillian and Babette seem more vivid to Erica than her actual friends.

Erica is given the details of their deterioration and she absorbs these fragments without effort. They arrange themselves, as if she has an innate capacity for this ordering. She understands these proportions, their facets, how they must be viewed and composed. She envisions Babette, the French skier, frail now, ninety-three pounds. Babette, who never married or had children, who chose instead an intimacy with mountains, a life of suitcases and hotels facing ridges of white, is now confined to a wheelchair.

Erica has memorized the saga of Lillian, shunned by her oncologist, left without a referral for three months, and finally sent to an experimental chemotherapy program. The doctor tells her they expect the treatment to fail.

In the long mornings of waxy stray sunlight across camellias, she finds herself waiting for Ellen to telephone, to recite the most recent conversations, to impart the medical data and the second and third opinions. How Lillian, only a year before the vice-president of a stock brokerage, a woman with two hundred and seventy-five employees, called in the pre-dawn, terrified. They had removed the plug from her arm. They wanted her to get out of bed and into a wheelchair.

"They're dismissing me, and I'm too sick to go home," Lillian realized and wept. "I'm afraid. I keep drifting off."

"What did you do?" Erica asks. She can see part of the street from her living room window. The leaves on the orange trees look artificial, landscaped beyond recognition. They are not trees, but someone's concept of how trees should look.

"I tracked down the resident. He said Lillian could die any minute. She doesn't have a month left." Her sister sounds broken. "I told him Lillian lives alone. I said he couldn't send her home alone, not like this."

She imagines Lillian, whom she has only met twice and cannot clearly remember, as a tall woman with white hair and a straw hat with yellow silk flowers. Now this Lillian is shrunken, ordered into a wheelchair and pushed to the front of a building she cannot recognize. She has no hair, she is too weak to fasten her wig, it's become too complicated. A nurse who barely speaks English—is from the Philippines or Guatemala—deposits the wheelchair at a curb where a taxi attempts to take Lillian to an apartment she cannot provide adequate directions to.

After all, north or south of Wilshire are an immensity of possibility, everything writhes, stung by citrus and pastel, who could draw the line? Lillian knows there are indications. Poinsettias in a cluster might be December. There are lilies at Easter. That comes in April. Of course vegetation is a kind of compass that rises from the ground. There is always a chorus of pigments. This is why we believe in resurrection. And Lillian couldn't get out of a taxi, walk across a lobby, wait for an elevator, open the many locks of the heavy front door she had insisted on. And there's no food there, there hasn't been food in weeks. She just eats through a plug. She can't remember how to turn on appliances or who she gave her cat to.

Erica wonders if these are parables. Is this what happens to women who dare to live alone, even the good ones, like Lillian, a churchgoer who doesn't sin, ever? Her sister is adamant. Lillian is from the South for God's sake, she wears gloves and gives money to an organization to protect stray animals.

The air smells scrubbed, polished, and detoxed. It is a winter that has been taught a lesson. And Erica doesn't want Flora to be left like this, in some remote time, when she can't be there to protect her, to make sure about release forms, wheelchairs, plugs, the administration of morphine, a bed with a view of the tops of palms, the secret avenues in the air where they open their fans and do their ancient naked dance that has nothing to do with love.

Suddenly Erica remembers when she decided to murder her daughter. They were living in northern California.

It was the winter it never stopped raining. It would be the coldest and wettest winter on record. She was going to graduate school and they didn't know anyone in the county. Erica was still smoking three packs of cigarettes a day. She had bronchitis again. It was her fourth bout of bronchitis that year and she refused to take a chest x-ray. The doctor in the student clinic said she was killing herself, pointed his long white arm at the door, placed her chart on the counter next to her purse, turned his back, walked away.

Erica was convinced she had lung cancer. She could sense the blue particles like a glacial stream, trickling and widening. The rain made them grow. They were sensitive to water. She could feel inside her veins to a fluid she imagined was the color of chilled larkspur. She was certain she wouldn't survive this California winter.

It was before she married Bob. She lay awake listening to the rain and considering her daughter Flora without her, a four-year-old orphan, a ward of the state. A child to be adopted by foster parents who would sexually abuse her, fail to provide piano lessons and poetry. A child to be raised in apartments where she was the entertainment for the brothers and uncles, and the television set was always on.

There was only one possible solution. She would take Flora into her bed, curve into her body, hold her beneath the quilt. They would both take sleeping pills and the winter would be over. But she didn't kill Flora that night, didn't kill herself, and now it is Los Angeles in early February.

Everything feels and tastes like spring. The afternoon dissolves into impressions, phantom images. We give them anchors, we give them language, she thinks. We practice acts of anthropomorphism, we wield the rules of grammar, but they are still creatures, pulsing.

She needs to see Flora. She is nine blocks from her school. It is afternoon and at 2:30 the fourth graders have gym on North Field. Erica can sit behind a clump of oleander and watch her daughter play volleyball near the fence. The day has become simple, transparent. She can either walk along the ocean or watch Flora move through lacquered sunlight. These are the only two indisputable activities in this world.

She walks past an orange tree, then a tree with lemons that look distended, and one with tangerines that are a sharp red. They would sting the mouth. You could bite into them and burn or bleed. You could serve such fruit at weddings or wakes. Yesterday she watched Bob pack. He was going to a meeting in Washington. He said she seemed different. "I'm fine. I'm perfectly fine," she had replied.

She remembers saying this to her mother. She had employed exactly the same cadence, the precise rise and fall of her voice like a series of bells in a plaza passed by in a speeding night train. This is a lie she has long ago engraved within herself. This is the way she imagines grown-ups speak. And her mother said, "Don't make me laugh."

"I'm getting myself together," she had told her mother. It might have been at the end of graduate school, during her first divorce. It might have been the winter she almost murdered her daughter.

"It's going to take you a lifetime," her mother said. Her mother was drinking vodka. She surveyed her coolly, evaluated her like a suit she didn't consider worth buying. Then she smiled.

Of course, her mother and father are dead now. They are dead but not quite gone. There is an entire substratum of people like this, people she doesn't quite know and yet they somehow linger. There is the matter of her sister with the two best friends who are dying. There are her daughter's mystery friends that surface and are erased, names she has never heard before suddenly brandished as best friends.

"You know Alexa?" Flora begins. Erica says, no. "Alexa, my best friend," Flora continues, highlighting each of her words, obviously annoyed.

This name is not familiar. She feels defensive and afraid. "I know Robin and Claudia," she reminds her daughter. "I know the twins. But not Alexa."

She is combing Flora's hair. It is night. She winds strands into tiny black braids. In the morning when the braids are undone, Flora will be adorned with vast complexities of curl. Now Flora looks like her head is a nest of snakes. We give birth to mythology over and over, Erica realizes, almost trembling with terror. We are the dried riverbeds where they hatch, where they drag their cold bodies across sand. It is from our bellies that they come.

"You're lying," Flora says. "All you do is talk on the phone. You don't even drive me to school anymore." Then she slams her bedroom door.

Now it is important that she find Flora and tell her she wasn't lying. There are protocols for the keeping of names. These syllables are sacred. When the winds have taken everything, even the buildings and the stones and the bark, these names will remain. These are the perpetually open graves. She is going to explain this to her daughter. She will defend herself against this suggestion of desecration.

Last night her sister called with more information about Babette. She can no longer sit. She has to sleep strapped to a board, upright, held by buckles. Her bones are turning to a kind of tin. Her sister cannot pronounce the name of the new disease. She can only say that Babette is rusting. She has nightmares filled with liquids, rain, waterfalls, a recurrent beach where she watches the approach of a tidal wave. Ellen has just visited her. She says Babette's skin smells like dust. She creaks when she breathes.

Erica knows both women were misdiagnosed, twice. Somewhere there are four mistakes and someone must be counting. Last night she asked her sister, "Do you ever talk to Lillian about death? About dying?" Erica was lying on her bed. She wanted to know. Bob had not yet gone to Seattle. Erica had shut her bedroom door.

Her sister thought for a moment. She said, "No."

"What do you talk about?" Erica asks.

"Ordinary things," her sister told her. "Who's playing good tennis. Who got a face-lift. Whose kid is in jail. The weather, the economy. You know."

Erica does know. When her father was dying, when he was decaying in front of them inches from their faces and almost in slow motion, it was the one thing no one ever spoke about. Father had the cancer stench. It was a kind of rancid yellow that made her think of tortured fruit and strange rotting cargoes abandoned at sea and something terrible done in rooms with unshaded lightbulbs, abortions, perhaps, or children being photographed naked. Her father's skin became translucent. He was a region of rivers. You could look inside and see his infinity of blue sins.

Erica wants to ask her sister if she remembers this but she doesn't. They never speak about their parents or the way they died or what their lives might have meant. Their parents simply disappeared, like a species that vanished overnight. It's as if they never were.

Erica realizes there is an entire ghost substratum inhabiting her. She's become aware of how much time she spends thinking about people she doesn't know and will never know, doesn't even want to meet once. Not just Lillian and Babette, these secondary tragedies she's internalized, not just Flora's profusion of suddenly found and lost best friends, but how she thinks about movie stars and European royalty and the state of their marriages.

She doesn't do this consciously, she would never permit herself to do this consciously. But when she takes her emotional pulse, when she looks directly inside, what she's been thinking about during a three-way traffic light, during a wait in a line at the bank, is Elizabeth Taylor and her new husband, the former carpenter and drug dealer. What do they do together? Do they attend AA meetings? Do they work the twelve-step recovery program? Do they promptly admit mistakes and answer crisis hotlines? She thinks they secretly drink and take drugs. Liz shows him what she has learned about pain pills and champagne. And he initiates her into the sordid avenues of hard-faceted white, the great internal winter, cocaine.

Now, during her leave of absence, when she can take her emotional pulse repeatedly with concentrated deliberation, she realizes she has been colonized by the insubstantial, something leaking, broken and generic out of the self-destructing culture. It's a kind of collective virus.

She used to think about Virginia Woolf and Sylvia Plath. That was when she lived with painters, when she lived in lofts above Indian restaurants and afternoons smelled of curry and the sun set in a sequence of saffrons, when she thought the bungalows behind hedges of sunflowers along the Venice canals were holy and her parents were not yet dead.

She didn't try to imagine Sylvia Plath and her husband in bed. She didn't envision Virginia wrapped in the arms of a woman, rain falling and what they might have done with their mouths. She visualized instead the kitchens where they brewed tea, the patterns of painted pink rosebuds on the cups, and the way the wind sounded as if it had just been eating ships. But the graphic couplings she now considers, the intricacies of bodies and proclivities, this she has saved for television stars.

It is 1:30 and she is four blocks from Flora's school. She can sense that Lillian is going into a coma. That's what Lillian was afraid of when she telephoned Ellen and wept, "Don't let them send me home. I feel like I'm drifting in and out."

Erica closes her eyes and there are acres of faces within her. She is even replete with the spouses of men she barely knows. How many afternoons had she imagined her lawyer's wife? She did this for months during her first divorce, staring at the photograph on his desk. A blond woman with ice skates balanced over her right shoulder. A woman wearing a green wool sweater and sunglasses. She was often tempted to ask her name. She finally decided it was Ingrid or Justine. She was good with dogs and gardens, never got migraines, enjoyed baking.

It occurs to Erica that what she wants to research is not history as it actually is or was, but some more fragile peripheral version, in its own way filled with untamed ambiguity. It would be a history of the undead, the flickering partials and the almost.

In these regions of ambivalence are the men she almost married. Erica has reconstructed pieces of their lives, a conversation, a newspaper clipping, an accidental sighting, something overheard. She might have stayed with Derek in Maui. Or the photographer in Spain. There are the lingering pulsings of these multiple almost-hers, standing on balconies of apartments and villas, watering geraniums, wearing a white slip above cobblestone alleys, above a plaza or a bay.

Jason, telephoning her at the university two years ago. She was working late. He was drunk. "I'm drinking fifteen-year-old scotch and it's been fifteen years since I fucked you. Come over."

Erica looked out her office window, noted the low soiled mountains and considered it. It was August in Southern California and everything seemed burned, even at night. It was the time of the avenues of scorch and the unraveling of an indelible yellow.

She could reach into the substrata of the barely known, make a date, meet in a motel in Long Beach, maybe, or in the Valley, Van Nuys, perhaps. It would have to be an urban suburb where no landscape could intrude, where it wouldn't be about beaches and palm trees, but California as it really was, back roads the color of mustard, smelling of onions and vinegar below hills where nothing could grow. In a valley of brush and sage and sand they could know the real nature of their hearts. It wasn't the stuff of postcards. But they knew this already. That's why she hung up.

We carry the undead with us, she thinks. That's why it's so hard to walk, why her boots hurt and the sun sears.

She still packs for Jason, still takes him to Hawaii and London with her. She stands at her closet, one closet or another, hearing him say, only red or black. You're a Toulouse-Lautrec whore. Anything else on your skin is an atrocity. And she finds herself repeatedly choosing these colors, in nightgowns and coats, tablecloths and socks.

Maybe she will tell her colleagues it is the history of the partial she wishes to explore, the terrain without specific intentions or borders. This is what she is thinking as she approaches Flora's school, as she sits on a lawn next to a rock with a bronze plaque nailed to it. "Dedicated to Maurice J. Finelander, 1918–1964." What did that forty-six-year-old man die from? Did he suffer, turn translucent, did he drift, could you look inside his chest and chart the avenues of his disgrace?

After she sees Flora, she will go home and wait for her sister to call. Afternoons are punctuated with desperate news about Lillian. Sometimes Erica telephones first. She has never called her sister so often, not even when their mother had a heart attack. They haven't spoken this often since they shared a room in the summer house.

"What's the latest with Lillian?" she will ask. Her eyes will be abnormally wide, she will take big breaths, as if there is some quality in the late afternoon wind that she requires.

Perhaps it has something to do with the enormous subterranean architecture she is discovering with its roots, shadows, and branching networks. This is beneath her feet all the time. This is what children sense under the bed. This is the secret structure of the world, and children feel this hidden spine. This is why they need stuffed pandas and teddy bears. This is why she has walked to the school to find her daughter, to tell Flora she would never lie about the names of the almost-known.

Suddenly, Erica recognizes a complexity that makes her decide to turn back. She wants to tell Flora that certain fragments seem like lies but they are not. It is simply the other world with its decaying possibilities casting luminous debris. It is not deliberate. There is no malice. But names get lost here. They are like seashells washed up on a wide night shore in a season of not enough moon. Inside each shell is a name, and the sea speaks it clearly, says Alexa, Flora, Lillian. But there are winds, the intrusion of partially forgotten winters that in memory are a stark and insinuating blue. And Erica realizes that she cannot tell this to Flora. This is a stretch of beach you must find for yourself and then only in a drowning season.

Erica walks home on a boulevard where the sidewalk is planted with rosebushes, bird-of-paradise, and iris, and she is thinking about events in the subterranean world. Here are the traffic accidents we almost had, but didn't.

Here are the planes we missed that might have carried bombs on them. Do the almosts form an architecture? Is that how you navigate in the cities of the undead?

Later that week, her sister calls, desperate. Lillian has run away. She's had a paranoid seizure, perhaps from the drugs, or maybe the cancer has metastasized into her brain. No one knows. She just took her raincoat and wallet and disappeared from the hospital. Her neighbor saw her get out of a cab. Lillian explained that she had come back for her cat.

"What should I do?" her sister Ellen asks.

She imagines her sister holding the phone, pacing, staring out the balcony. The wind has been blowing, a Santa Ana from the desert. Everything seems a form of fleshy yellow. It is a night of skin. Lamps are insignificant. The moon is so inordinately bright she thinks the savannah must have been like this, rocked by streaks of yellow with the intensity of seduction and prophecy.

"We'll drive the streets and find her," Erica decides. "I'll pick you up."

Flora has suddenly appeared. She is always barefoot, soundless. She simply materializes. She is holding her math book open at her hip. Flora could survive in the night,

with her head of uncoiling snakes. She seems to be waiting for something. Erica knows what her daughter is doing. Flora is stalking.

Bob has returned from his conference in Seattle. He is
staring at her, watching her assemble car keys, wallet,
jacket, watch. He studies the objects she is sliding into her
pockets as if he plans to collect evidence. He is standing in
front of the living room door as if he intends to guard it.

Earlier, when she was cooking dinner, Bob asked if she
had gone to the library. He had telephoned and she
wasn't home. She said no. She stared at the cheese she
was cutting. She examined the tip of the knife. Her husband didn't understand that she was never going back to
the library. It didn't contain the artifacts she needed. Then
he asked what she had done all day.

"I don't remember," she said. She was holding a knife.
It felt hard in her hand. She put it down. She could feel
the moon through the window. It occurred to her that
there was no history, only the etiology of yellow.

Now Bob says, "Where are you going?"

There is always this moment, she realizes. The where
and the why. The demand for coordinates and specifics,
the number of acres, who saw the troops, which direction
and how many. There is always this and the way sometimes you don't answer.

"It's Lillian," she says, walking quickly toward the door.
He is heavier but he has trouble with his knees. She could
outflank him if she had to. "She's roaming the streets.
She's lost her mind."

Erica considers the invisible artifacts she has recently
unearthed. She thinks about mapping the subterranean
strata. What sort of tools would she need, what form of
illumination?

"But you don't even know that woman," her husband
says.

"I do know her," Erica replies. "I've never known anyone so well."

Flora is staring at her. They look into one another's eyes and Erica realizes communication is dimensional, like something knitted, a rope or a net. Then she is walking into the yellowed night where the wind sounds like a rushing river, there is a lashing of branches, and the leaves are clinging to stay on.

guerrilla noon

Her mother, Veronica, comes to her house for lunch. It is Lindsay's forty-second birthday. Lindsay doesn't think her mother can do it, have a simple salad and not try to break her heart.

It's been raining for days, an unusual northern storm turned south, virulent with stray thunder. The gray looks thick and permanent. The city seems oddly incomplete, unformed, washed out. It could be a movie set struck, used, and collectively abandoned.

Lindsay has had enough psychotherapy to understand that her mother is emotionally crippled. But Veronica is not sick enough to put into a hospital. She dwells in a cyclic domain where she will never get substantially better or worse. Her particular pathology does not require a structured intervention of any kind. If she had to hold a job, she probably could not. But Veronica will never have to work.

Her mother is a borderline neurotic. She's a sort of guerrilla in her own shifting frontier, raiding, savaging, not bothering with a flag. It is possible Veronica inhabits an area that existed at the beginning of human time when the myths had not yet coalesced. It was an era when there was only hunger, sharp objects, and no larger context. One was always naked and kept embers and caches of throwing stones.

"Jesus. Stop playing the ingenue," Zak said. "Meet her in a public place. Meet her in the police station."

Later Lindsay telephoned her mother with a list of possible restaurants. Veronica appeared to be considering suggestions. Then she said they were boring.

"You never could pick a restaurant," Veronica said. "And I know what you're doing. You don't want me in your house. You're a dime novel. You're transparent. What do you think I'll do? Leave a yellow puddle where I sit?"

Lindsay was nearly a month over deadline. She had been working past midnight for weeks. She felt too exhausted to argue. There would be no point in explaining her schedule to Veronica. Her mother did not have a vocabulary that included the concept of personal danger through excess. Veronica's idea was that you did as much as you could, and when you couldn't do any more, you dropped dead. There were no gradations.

Lindsay listened to the rain. She experienced a certain trepidation about her mother's impending visit. She felt she couldn't get enough air. She hadn't been herself the afternoon before, had in fact argued with Zak on the tennis court.

"I told you to buy new balls," Zak said. They were standing in the parking lot of the community center where they played tennis several evenings a week.

"These are fine," Lindsay said. She held one yellow ball in the palm of her hand.

"Fine?" Zak repeated. He grabbed the ball and bounced it once. "What's your plan? Play with them until they dial 911?"

"I'm sorry," Lindsay said. She didn't feel sorry, only a vast gray that reminded her of cotton candy. The sky was fat with rain. It looked like it was choking.

Zak stared at her. "It's your mother, isn't it?"

Lindsay said no. Then she played badly. She felt queasy

at dinner. Later, close to a dawn that never separated it-self from the gray, she had thrown up.

That night she had the rat dream and the dog dream. She has the rat dream recurrently, in intricate variations of geography, seasons, and architecture. The fundamental plot is the same. She lives in an enormous house with rats in it. This knowledge is something she avoids, denies the meaning of the darting black shapes, the scurrying she senses near her bare ankles. She doesn't have shoes. She wakes, feeling she has been violated somehow while she slept. It has something to do with animals, being chased or being eaten. At first she thinks it must be coyotes or wild dogs. Only slowly does the absolute certainty of rats enter her.

In the morning, minutes before Veronica rings her doorbell, Zak telephones. "Any blood yet?" he asks. And softer, "What's wrong?"

Lindsay says, "I'm just a little foggy." She means she is having trouble breathing. She means she can sense Veronica approaching.

Zak is a mathematician and he believes in logic and a world where things are or are not. And if they are not, they are discarded. He does not understand why this old woman, who is obviously mentally ill, exerts so vast a force upon her.

Then her mother is at the door. Lindsay notices the shopping bag filled with wrapped department store boxes, and she experiences a terrific rush of unease. Ordinarily, Veronica does not give presents. It's as if she occupies some terrain of near starvation where the idea that anyone would receive a gift for any reason is simply unthinkable. One can conceive of a sweater, perhaps, some tinder for starting a small fire, one potato and a thin branch, but that's as far as it goes. Of course, Veronica's purchasing affliction only concerns other people. She is perfectly capable of shopping for herself.

As if following the trajectory of her eyes, Veronica says,

"Those aren't for you. I give you too much already. I just didn't want to leave them in the car."

Lindsay can comprehend the inflection in her mother's voice. There is the intimation that this street where she lives is too shabby, too dangerous for her mother's recent purchases. And it occurs to Lindsay that what she feels for her mother is so beyond embarrassment it almost lacks a category.

She is watching her mother stand in the doorway of her house. Veronica has just returned from Miami. The reason for her visit has nothing to do with Lindsay's birthday. Veronica simply wants to show off her suntan.

"I have to demo this before it fades," Veronica had said on the telephone. "This needs a demo. You've got to see my legs."

Okay, Lindsay thought. Okay. Lindsay has decided that being an adult is like being a circus juggler. You're in the middle of a gouged circle of rancid sawdust and somebody is shining a spotlight in your eyes while someone else keeps tossing you more plates. And when you conclude there is no possible way to choreograph one more spinning disk of china, there can be no more sleight of hand, that's when another plate is tossed right at you, eye level. Today, the plate is named Veronica. And Lindsay knows her mother is going to spoil her birthday.

"There's a terrible smell in here," Veronica began. She paused in the doorway. She scanned the living room as if expecting to discover small carcasses, perhaps from rodents or mounds of something worse. There are implications in her look. Wherever her daughter is, there are unclean practices, impurities, stains.

"I don't know what it could be," Lindsay said, quickly. She feels as if she is falling, and she is frightened. "There are only those flowers on the piano."

She wants her mother to tell her the camellias and roses and geraniums she has grown in her backyard and arranged in the vase are beautiful. She knows Veronica won't say this.

"It could be anything. I'm so sensitive. I had to change my plane seat four times," Veronica tells her. She isn't looking at the vase of flowers. They are gone and they never happened. "You know how I am."

Veronica decides to enter the house. She is holding a piece of paper in her right hand. Lindsay recognizes it as the dividend Veronica has been giving her four times a year since Justin was born. Now Veronica waves the paper in the air between them and says, "This is the last one you get."

Lindsay stares at her mother. She feels her mouth opening, as if to gasp for air or bite something. She sometimes has the sensation that she actually wants to lunge forward and remove the skin from her mother's face with her teeth. She remembered Zak saying, "She's going to renege. She's setting you up. Don't trust her."

"But you agreed to give me this," Lindsay pointed out. "I quit my job. I'm only free-lancing now." She has learned how to sound reasonable. This has taken years. Now she feels herself slump back against the bookcase, her knees shake, she is vaguely nauseous.

"I never made an indefinite promise," Veronica said. She was studying the surface of an end table as if for dust or fingerprints or other tangible signs of neglect. "A few months to help you out when you married the genius with no money. That's all I said. A few months."

This was not the truth. Lindsay tried to assemble a framework of assurances and agreements, a grid of words and dates. She could remember what Veronica had said and when. She could recall the weather, the time of day, and what her mother had been wearing. Lindsay could create an architecture from this in miniature detail, scaled like the model of a city. But her mother would say it was meaningless. She would say it had never happened.

"I get nothing for this money," Veronica informed her. "I'd make a meal out of a morsel but you don't drop a crumb."

Lindsay looked at the floor. The rain was hitting the

roof harder now, and it made her think of bells and the inscriptions on cathedrals in Europe and the neon on motels along American highways. She thought of childhood and distilling it to a single image, and that would be one tree in rain, an oak.

"I can tell how much you hate me. You hate every molecule in my body. You've said that to me a hundred times," Veronica told her.

Lindsay considered the pattern on her snakeskin boots. They were red and black, and Zak had given them to her for her birthday. They had a complicated pattern of flowers and hearts carved into the leather that began at the calf. She was thinking that Veronica had never understood science. Molecules were too vast and complex, with their sequences and structures. They didn't explain her hate at all.

Lindsay remembered a high-school essay she had written on whether it was immoral to murder someone you didn't know by simply pressing a button. If you could push a sort of buzzer in absolute secrecy, and some stranger in Argentina or China would die, and you would get a million dollars, would you do it?

Her class had split roughly fifty–fifty between the murderers and nonmurderers. She had, of course, said the act was immoral. But now, twenty-five years later, she realizes if she could kill Veronica and not be traced she would do it. She had told this to Zak.

"I could only endorse that if the death involved torture," Zak had said.

Now Lindsay glances at her mother. The suddenness with which Veronica removed her financial support had taken her by surprise. Lindsay assumed they were in a period of thaw. It was cyclic, of course, fragile and without recognizable boundaries. Nonetheless, she had not expected the cruelties between them to resume precisely on her birthday.

She managed to see Veronica on Thanksgiving. Zak had taken them to a restaurant. He sat next to her mother, who drank two bottles of wine and didn't seem to notice that she and Justin were also at the table. Zak had deemed the evening a success.

During the Christmas holidays, she and Zak and Justin go camping in the desert. They do this so Veronica can't reach them by phone, threaten to take an overdose or call repeatedly drunk. It is during Christmas that her mother develops strange transitory diseases, a blindness in one eye that lasts a week, an inability to bend from the waist, a pain in her head she insists is a brain tumor. There is no place safe from Veronica during the holidays unless it is somewhere without electricity. They have learned how to do this, camp in the Anza Borega Desert or the Baja. They have sleeping bags rated for below zero. They have emergency rations, flares, tarps, and a .357 Colt. They go camping even in storms.

Once Lindsay had seen Veronica accidentally. They had run into each other on the jogging path along Santa Monica Boulevard, and this had produced an unauthorized spontaneous visit. That had lulled Lindsay into believing the thaw was still in effect and might remain so. Now she realizes Veronica has returned from Miami prepared for acts of war. Veronica has come back refreshed, with heightened blood lust.

Lindsay feels shaken. She looks outside. She thinks the rain is a sort of time traveler. It doesn't care about centuries or inventions. It opens its arms and speaks in a language of orchids and volcanoes, green doves and chants. Rain falls in the courtyards and plazas, and they are enclosed by radiance. The rain is foreign. It comes from antiquity, and when it falls on cities or faces or ruins, they are blessed, transcendent.

Lindsay remembered when Zak asked, "Why don't you just never see her again?"

She had attempted to explain this to him. He looked unconvinced. He had gone to college when he was seventeen. His father told him not to call home until he changed his major to law. Zak had literally never spoken to his family again. Zak understood the resolution of numbers and how they were a language and a port you could sail from, but he did not comprehend psychological time. He believed character was a matter of will and discipline. He thought he was the same age as the man on his driver's license.

It had all been different for her, but she felt too tired to open her mouth, to assemble and articulate her reasons, why she had selected one juncture and not some other. Her definitions seemed vague and insubstantial. They were experiments she couldn't repeat, replicate, publish the data. She felt as if she was looking into someone else's life.

It had been night then and also raining. The moon was tarnished behind banks of cloud. She thought it was possible that the clouds formed a species of Braille. She could open the window and touch them.

"If it wasn't for this money, you'd never see me at all," Veronica said.

Lindsay realized that her knees were shaking. They were standing in the living room with a scent of wild iris and camellias just pulled from the rain. Her mother thought this was peculiar.

"Look at this." Veronica pointed to the yellow streamers that criss-crossed the room, hung from the light fixtures and the top of the stairs. Zak and Justin had woken at 5 A.M. to hang her party decorations. She had discovered an oversized balloon printed with *Happy Birthday, Mom* taped on her bedroom door. In the living room she had found wrapped gifts.

"You don't think of asking me to your party, do you? Your own mother." Veronica lit a cigarette. She studied the streamers with what might have been surprise or contempt.

"I don't ask you to my birthday because I know you'll spoil it. I'm trying to protect you from yourself. From doing something irrevocable in front of Zak or Justin," Lindsay said.

The cigarette smoke burned her eyes. She had repeatedly told Veronica that no one could smoke in their house. They didn't even have ashtrays. Veronica ignored her, put out cigarettes in plants and tossed them in the sink. Lindsay would find their dried bodies for days, like a trail of reptiles, of shed skins, desiccated corpses. If she confronted Veronica, her mother would deny having smoked in her house. Veronica would say she would never do such a thing. Lindsay looked at her mother. "I think you better leave now," she said.

"Because you got your bucks?" Veronica made a spitting gesture with her lips. "You got the bucks so now you can throw the broad out?"

Lindsay noticed that she was edging further away from her mother. She was retreating. They had started in the living room, backed through the dining room, and now they were standing in the middle of the kitchen. Soon she would be cornered.

Lindsay recognized that she was employing primate postures of fear and submission. She was leaning against the kitchen door, her back pressed to the cold wood, and she was cringing. Her arms hung limply at her sides, her palms were raised as if beseeching a benediction. Then she opened the refrigerator and blindly began to eat. She picked up a stick of butter and gnawed on it.

"You think I'm over the hill," Veronica accused. "I saw more in one off-season than you'll see in your whole pathetic life. Bow-wow. Bow-wow. Look in the mirror. You're a bow-wow."

"Tell me when you take your best shot. I wouldn't want to miss it," Lindsay said. "Was that it?"

The entire tenor of Veronica's voice altered. She tossed her cigarette into the kitchen sink. Her face suddenly softened. It was as if somewhere the lighting cues had changed.

"I'm an old woman. I'm all alone," Veronica began. She seemed stunned, as if she has just admitted this for the first time. "Everybody hates me. I've been shunned. I've been betrayed in ways you can't imagine. People I loved ran away. I could die in my house and no one would know until the smell hit the street."

Veronica often said that, about dying in the house alone. It was one of her favorite conversational pieces. She thought her mother must have seen this event in a movie, perhaps on an airplane.

Lindsay closed her eyes. The rain was a form of wave. It was an ancient caress. It came from the ocean and then rustled the lemon and avocado trees. It fell on the grass in the cemeteries, it fell on the flower shops and cafés and ferns. It flowed through the city streets like a river, eternal like thunder and murder.

"You've told me how you feel about me on my birthday," Lindsay said. "I've heard enough now." She was still leaning against the wall. She was crouched. She had eaten half a stick of butter.

"You look like you need a drink," Veronica said. "I need one, too. Pour something."

"I don't drink," Lindsay replied. Her voice sounded as if it was coming from an impossible distance, from beyond the known rivers and oceans. Her voice seemed blue and unusual. She thought about geological strata relentlessly unfolding. She considered stars above jungle flowers in rain and how they were both aberrations, one grounded and one floating.

"No drinky today? What about the other stuff. The shoot-it-up? That's what you like. Shoot-it-up. You got any?" Veronica stared at her. "That's always the threat with you. You've always got that axe hanging over this old broad's neck, don't you?"

Lindsay turned away from her mother. It occurred to her that thoughts were never really finished. They fanned outward, like cities, their resonance a slow spiral. In the end, there were only books bound in leather, pianos played by children, and candles on mahogany tables. There was rain and moon and wild iris. There were variations. Sometimes there were gardens and bridges. And it had been nearly eleven years since she had taken a drink.

"That's it," Veronica clapped her hands together. "You're a junky again. You need my money to shoot it up. Shoot it up. I'm waiting. Everybody knows. All your teachers. Then the social workers."

Rain fell across her patio, on the begonias and geraniums she had planted in pots. She had taken cuttings from purple geraniums on the cliffs north of Malibu. They were hiking in a late spring. At the end of the trail they had found a sort of cove of crushed wild grasses. Zak said deer had been sleeping there. They had placed Justin down in the moist green weeds. She had wanted to remember the moment. That's why she took a piece of flower. Now the rain seems a sullen silver, the color of broken solitude and women who stand at windows alone. "I can't eat lunch after this," Lindsay said.

"Throw the broad out now that you got the bucks. You'll die with a needle in your arm like a whore. That's the statistics. Ninety-nine out of a hundred die with the needle in the vein. That's how you'll go," Veronica noted. She seemed calm.

There was something in her mother's tone that made her lose her composure. Or perhaps it was a new alignment, a shifting not of solar bodies but of people in rooms. They, too, had their orbits and their gravities. And of course her legs would move. She could stand upright. Evolution began with an idea, Lindsay understood that. First there was the concept, then one designed legs and tools, vehicles, quiet boulevards, harbors and history. We are always struggling to crawl up on land, breathe air. And she could walk out of the kitchen. She could cross the living room and open the front door. She was going to do that.

"You never ask me anything about my life," Veronica suddenly said, her voice soft, somehow muted, almost moist. "Nothing about my trip. It's like I don't exist. It's like I'm already dead. Well, I'll tell you anyway. I don't like Miami. Florida's a sucker play. It's second rate. It's for old people. The streets are shabby. It's nothing like Los Angeles. You know what else? The people are trash. They're inbreds. Half the couples you see on those squalid beaches aren't even husbands and wives. It's brothers and sisters. Incest is big-time down there. Trailer parks. Bingo. Cold cuts and that Americana crap that comes in plastic bags. Chips. Peanuts. You could throw the garbage at them. They'd stand up on their back legs to catch it. It's a zoo."

Lindsay thought there was something luminescent in the rain. It reminded her of pewter and lime trees and longing. That is what we are filled with, longing. That is what lights the faces of people caught on buses and subways, in their startled half-lives.

Veronica was doing something. She was removing an object from her black canvas bag printed with *Cannes* in red block letters. She had taken out a kind of book. It looked like a ledger.

"I write everything down," Veronica informed her. "Everything. Phone messages. Mail. This is for my lawyer. Last winter, five weeks, I didn't get a single telephone call." Veronica looked at her. "You never phoned. Not once. And you want my money?" Veronica seemed to be studying the edge of her shoe. "You know why there's no one to hold me now? You destroyed all my marriages. No man wanted a broad with a junky for a daughter."

Lindsay remembers one particular psychiatrist at the last of the many hospitals she was taken to. She had stopped using drugs. In two years, she would meet Zak and then Justin would be born. It was afternoon. She was in her doctor's office. He had said, "I'm going to tell you something. I want you to take this in and I think you can. If your mother ever saw herself as she truly is, it would require an act of immediate suicide on her part."

"Why so sad?" Veronica asked. "Thought I'd stay in Miami permanently? You'd just get a check in the mail? No old broad to grease? You'd like that big-time, I know. You'd like me in Florida with some old geezer with a nitro patch and a dick he jacks up with a bicycle pump. That's not my style."

It's been more than a decade since Lindsay used drugs. She suddenly recognizes that it is this version of herself, this incarnation that Veronica remembers and cherishes. This is when they were closest. This is when her mother felt needed. It was in the era of ambulances, in the time of the constant shivering. This is when her mother felt loved.

Lindsay has bought Veronica a pair of sterling silver earrings shaped like hearts. She had planned to say they were a token of the gratitude she felt for Veronica having made her born. She wants to say this but she cannot. The space where that sentence would have gone has been soldered shut. There are always caskets in the long noons, there are the burials that barely register and no one sends flowers.

Now Lindsay reaches into her pocket and silently offers the tiny heart-shaped box to her mother. Veronica stares at it with distaste. Then she removes the lid as if expecting the worst.

"I don't wear that kind of clasp," Veronica says, holding the earrings in her palm, evaluating them from two angles. "That's a clasp for hillbillies. That's what they sell in Florida. Jesus, it looks like a fishing hook. Real jewelry is always studs. You got conned. You never learn. I could have taught you everything, too." Veronica closes the box and places it on the kitchen counter. She would not put such a pair of earrings in her black canvas bag with *Cannes* printed on the side. It might contaminate her.

"You never touch me," Veronica suddenly said. She is using her hurt voice, the one with the many broken tones like a cargo of spilled bells on the bottom of the ocean. They are no longer in the kitchen. Lindsay has had an insight into the nature of evolution. They are on the edge of the living room. They are moving toward the front door. Lindsay recognizes this as an inevitability. "Not a hand on my shoulder, not lips on my cheek. You look at me like I was radioactive. How do I feel? An old woman longing for the touch of another human being. Just my wrist, just my hand."

Lindsay reached across space and her fingers found the doorknob. She turned it and the door opened. There are laws of cause and effect, she thought. Rituals of purification. Proclamations that do not vanish. There are the pink of camellias and the sudden streaks of wild iris.

Then she touched her mother's shoulder. She squeezed her hands into her mother's silk suit jacket as if attempting to tattoo the fiber of her skin. "I have a take-home message for you," Lindsay said. "I don't hate you on a molecular level. That's trivial. My hatred is deeper. Think subatomic. And get out."

Lindsay will tremble for two days. She will dream about rats and her hands will shake and then it will be over, but only for then. Now there is something she must understand. That is why she is watching her mother out the living room window. There is some yellowed gauze in the air, if only she could decode it.

Veronica is smoking a cigarette and slowly walking between the avocado and lemon trees as if she was taking a sort of tour. She is following not the redwood path but rather staking her own on the new fresh grass. The heels of her shoes are digging in like she was trying to hurt the earth or perhaps something fragile just beneath it.

Her mother is getting into her Mercedes-Benz. It is still noon. This is the hour when her mother and all the mothers go stalking scarves and gloves on sale at Neiman Marcus. They are in the aisles at Saks Fifth Avenue. They are there at the perfume counter where the spectrum flows from lilac to musk and there are always samples if you know how to ask. They are there in an oasis of aqua and turquoise, cobalt and midnight eye shadows. They are rustling amongst powders the colors of crushed iris. Here the lipsticks run in schools and swarms and streams of crimsons and vermillions, and sometimes they slide an eight-hundred-dollar enameled compact into their coat pocket.

Then they walk out to their car, which is parked beside a painted red curb. They take a sip of brandy from an antique silver flask they keep hidden in the locked dash. They smoke cigarettes and marijuana from the mountains of Mexico that their workout instructors and masseurs sell them.

The red lines painted on the curb have nothing to do with them. Or putting change in the parking meter. Or the go-slow warnings or pedestrian crossings or any of the predictable things cities try to tell them. They drive as fast as they want. And sometimes they get to take a cruise from Miami to Barbados just because he likes their face and the freckles on their angular legs. Sometimes they get to keep the stock, the house with the tennis court, the boat with their name on the side. And the signs that read *no shoplifting, no swimming, no smoking, no drinking, no bare feet, no volleyball after 9 P.M.* are insignificant.

You see them leaning back in their imported cars where the air is glazed and different. There is always music playing. They know the nature of time and who the rules were made for. They know it is a permanent stalled guerrilla noon. It is always the color of chartreuse silk, of sunflowers, of clusters of tiny hand-embroidered daisies, and they are chameleons, faster than you imagine. They have the energy of centuries of solitary Sundays when they conceived and perfected sabotage and seduction. You could never catch them. They are the jaguars of hit and run. They are what makes the orchids tremble. It is them, not the thunder.

the woman after rain

It is a day after rain and it is fiercely beautiful. From her bedroom window the colors are vivid, aggressive, almost violent. It is impossible to imagine them any other way. They might be from an era before tarnish or corruption. They have a depth beyond even the superimposed and painted way postcards of the desert or tropics look.

"They called me Mad Max way before the movie," her husband is saying.

It is a strange and stalled morning. It has the quality of internalized steam, she decides, the way jungle noons do. Max has brought her breakfast in bed, carried a tray with a carafe of coffee and a pink napkin covering a plate of toast with strawberry jam. There are white geraniums in a bud vase. He has learned to do this from her.

The idea that one could receive breakfast with an aesthetic component had never occurred to him before they met. This has always seemed an odd deletion, an omission that demands clarification. She wants to inquire further but she will not. We are like audio tapes with borders of static, edges where the unspeakable spilled and there are long and stinging silences. Certain events cannot be reconstructed. They have contrived to vanish, and we must let them go.

"I've been thinking about Knitter," Max said.

He sat on the bed and began talking about Knitter, who used to spend nights spool-knitting multicolored strings and then sewing the thumb-fat snakelike coils into round rugs. When they got back to base, Knitter cut a circle in the top and called them ponchos. He believed they were works of art, and he wanted hundreds of dollars for each one, cases of Scotch and bags of marijuana. He was addicted to knitting, took his yarns on search-and-destroy missions. Knitter would lean back against a tree and begin moving his needles through the thick green that seemed more a river than air.

When Knitter was killed, they divided up the ponchos and Max ended up with fifteen. He still has all of them. They smell of mothballs and the passage of time, if time is a sequence of hallucinations and decay, the repetition of a certain bridge falling, the same mountain burning, and some taint she has not been able to sun dry or soak out. Julia keeps the ponchos in a drawer, separate from other garments with bunches of potpourri, but the threads are immune. They want to smell of cul-de-sac rivers of green rot, and twenty years later they still do.

In this manner, Knitter did not completely die. Julia remembers a screen painting she saw in a museum in Taiwan. It was a simple river reed done in muted overcast grays, and it was completely covered with what Max told her were stamps. Each stamp was the name of an emperor's flunky, each inspector stamped the masterwork before he passed it on. In the end, their names were entwined with the painting. In time, the bureaucracy became art.

Now Julia is eating toast and Max is explaining methods of cooking on a search-and-destroy mission. He would take a piece of C-4 plastic explosive, place it in an old rations can that had holes punched in the side, and set it on fire. That was how you made a stove when you were on patrol and it was raining.

"That's dinner in the triple canopy," Max told her.

He was talking about the jungle with its three separate tiers and multiplicity of heat like invisible singed latitudes. She imagines this jungle as a kind of trapeze in a vast and curious circus where barelegged women swing. They are young, the age of her daughter, and they are named for flowers and gods and rare qualities of the soul, and they are always hungry.

Julia has a wood tray resting on her lap. In ten minutes her husband has an appointment with a doctor who will give him his biopsy report. Outside she can see Los Angles after a week of rains. This is what happens when the heartbreak has been washed away, the bad dreams and bad drugs, the pollution and chemicals, tragedy and miscalculation. This is how Los Angeles is cleansed. The storms must be sudden. You must take this city by surprise, by ambush.

"When I go, I'll go singing like Opera Man," Max said.

Opera Man was in Max's platoon. He was trained as a tenor and he was supposed to perform in Milan. Then Opera Man began to realize that every day was a performance, the set was perpetually viridescent, the curtains opened and fell on inspired cue, and the peripheral characters really died. He began to appreciate the terrarium stage with the intricacy of dome one could never comprehend. The stars at night were the least of it.

Opera Man sang arias on the trails beneath the three-tiered canopy. He sang for the terrarium in German or French or Italian, depending on the position of the moon. There were congruencies between lunar shape and pitch, what a crescent or a full moon demanded, how this could be translated into human tones. The last time her husband saw Opera Man, he was wearing one of Knitter's ponchos and singing for spare change in the Oakland Greyhound bus station.

Julia glances at her husband. Max is wearing jeans and a navy-blue sweat shirt with *Berkeley* written on it in yellow letters. She has heard his Vietnam stories before, and others, hundreds of times. They have never seemed comprehendible to her, seem almost an extension of his childhood, what happened after Little League. It is something else with boys, noise and blood and not getting caught. But this part of the tale is greener. It occurs to her that these jungle anecdotes are a kind of loop Max falls into when he is afraid. It is similar to the way some people cough or have a tic. This insight terrifies her. Max is going to see his internist and he is going alone.

Julia stands at the window and watches her husband drive away. She dresses quickly and walks back and forth across their front yard. This is their perimeter. There are no imperfections in the burnt adobe orange. The house is set behind a wrought-iron fence completely enclosed by ivy and geraniums and iris. The house looks somehow camouflaged. It could belong to anyone. The red geraniums, the white azaleas, the maple she had insisted on, this could have been landscaped by a stranger.

Of course anyone can walk out an oak door, follow a brick path to a street named for a tree, open a wire gate and cross a curb and there is no guarantee you will ever return. That's why Max woke her with Vietnam stories. All walks are patrols, search-and-destroy missions where we find and lose pieces of ourselves.

Julia has been waiting nearly a week for her husband's medical test results. The waiting had seemed bearable while it was raining. Now that the sun has reappeared, the moments seem sharper, longer, more finely etched, more like acid than silver.

The morning has been washed of everything, including ambiguity. There are no sullen corners. Above the street where she and Max have somehow come to live there are the slowly spreading chartreuse of jacaranda trees that make her think of veils and umbrellas, Paris and marriage at the beginning of time when surely you would paint your face with green. It would happen beside a river, the deflowering, then the official statements and payment, the trading of the woman for two oxen, perhaps, a bag of salt and a few seashells.

It is a morning of facets and angles. Ivy grows in the shape of perfect hearts with veins that pump in and out. The canna on the lawn near the gate feels greasy like skin when she touches it. Farther along the street, stalks are assembling in confederations that will become yellow-and-purple iris. Later sun will take their blossoms and starch and harden them like cheap hospital linen.

Today Max's doctor will probably tell him that he does not have a condition requiring surgery or chemotherapy or radiation. The inconclusive tests have proved to be a defect with the machinery. This has happened to both of them before. Something registered on the computer for no reason. Perhaps someone's hand shook. A lab tech spilled something. The girl on the phone had a headache. There was a tremor in Alpha Centuri and it chanced to pass through his body just as the x-ray did. There was a bubble on the film but it had nothing to do with him. It was the reflection of a distant moon in an unorthodox transit. It was possible someone in a nearby hotel was having a recurrent nightmare about fire. There are always inexplicable circumstances. The wrong tag on a bottle. The misplaced file.

Julia can see the medical towers three miles east from the house where anyone could live. It is a morning like any other except she excused herself from Ariel's car pool and her husband may have a terminal disease. It occurs to her that she could walk to the doctor's office. She could meet Max there. She could wait in the lobby below, deciphering something in the angle of his shoulders, in the way shadows might cling to his face as he exits the elevator. She would know.

Then Julia is walking. It's the end of another pretend California winter. It's the grand finale where a mock spring pushes out azaleas so thick they seem coated with pink snow. Bird-of-paradise rise on stalks and look poised and alert and alive. When the breeze shakes them they might be craning their necks or preparing to fly. Their movements are fluid and direct like predators.

Last night Max told her that he was with Opera Man and two others in San Francisco. It was after they were discharged. They needed to go to Santa Cruz and only had enough money for two bus tickets. It was winter and they drew straws. Max and another man lost, had to walk a hundred miles in the wind. They walked through the night and the next day. They never felt tired or cold. Every half hour Max took three more amphetamines, a sip of rum, and kept going.

Julia knows Max is speaking in code. He is telling her that she must keep going. But she has already deviated, failed to car pool, telephoned the other mother and said she had a problem. Julia called it a small scheduling conflict. This other mother wants Julia to commit herself to being a field-trip leader next week when the fourth-grade class visits Olvera Street in the heart of downtown Los Angeles. They will tour the first adobe mission, see a film about tile-making, and eat Mexican food. This is how they are going to learn the history of their state.

We are all learning the history of our state, Julia thinks. That's why Max told her about walking in the rain to Santa Cruz. That was forty-eight hours when he learned something about the history of his state.

"I'll have to look at my calendar. I'll have to call you back," Julia had said.

She has learned that this is how adults talk. They don't say, I'll be a field-trip leader unless my husband is having a section of his liver removed that day. No, the correct response is, I will check my schedule and get back to you. We are all learning the history of our state and when someone says how are you, the universally accepted answer is fine. We operate on a grid where complete sentences are unnecessary. In fact, they are offensive. It is the age of the password. Fine.

Julia studies the boulevard ahead of her. Each vine of ivy and thatch of bougainvillea is vivid and perfected.

Such clarity is only possible on days when you think someone you love may die. There is always the recurrence of this irony and paradox. We see that rain is a form of silver, of pewter and pearl we were meant to wear on our necks and in our hair only when we wait for our husband's biopsy. Max has told her there is a magnified clarity just before dawn and the firing of shots, when you walk the mud trail looking for the invisible wires of booby traps.

Julia is half a mile from the hospital and the twin towers with the doctor's offices, and the sidewalks are crowded with husbands and wives, children with aged parents. What proportion of them have flu or colds? How many with sprains, sore throats or injuries from tennis? Or do they have just a touch of something more complex and lethal? Are they waiting for the death report in the blood test or x-ray?

We have always lived like this. That's what Max would say. It's always been a form of lottery, who goes out in the storm to fish that day, who gets to stay home and repair nets. Who says I'll remain in camp with the children when they know they'll be alone with only one knife and a small pile of throwing stones. This is how we learn the history of our state. Some get chosen for patrol, some are left alone.

At the corner of a boulevard with a fan palm and an outdoor café, Julia is astounded by a tree with buds like pink fists, not the severed hands of children or angels but some more fragile species. She pulls a blossom from a branch, rubs it against her face, and the fragrance is pink and drunken. Clearly, it is meant to be opened and distilled, licked and bathed in. And there is still pyracantha near a bamboo fence where three slow maples are turning burgundy. It is the end of February in Los Angeles and it is all seasons simultaneously.

We must recognize these confluences, she decides, these repetitions of cycles. Julia is walking toward the hospital where ten years ago, almost precisely, her daughter was born. She will enter the same building. Now she will find out if there has been a mechanical error in her husband's medical report, some not-uncommon malfunction with one of the multimillion-dollar machines, or some problem with the person bending over the dial. There is always the matter of human error.

They didn't think Ariel was going to be born then. They said it was too soon. It was a full moon in winter. It had been raining. The doctor told her not to bring her bag, the one with the extra nightgowns, slippers, hairbrush, and paperback *Anna Karenina* that had been sitting by the front door for two months.

"Take the bag," she told Max. "I'm in labor or I'm dying from something else. Either way, check me in."

Ariel was born sixteen hours later, three minutes before midnight. Max took a photograph of the full moon above the hospital parking lot. He stood on the roof in a T-shirt getting soaked. Julia remembered that ten-year-old image last night. There was a full moon above their backyard. It looked like an unnatural veil across the swimming pool. She thought this was how water was buried.

It was raining lightly. Max was sitting with his feet in the tarnished cold swimming-pool water talking about Da Nang. It had suddenly become clear to her that we live moon-to-moon, always. We are pagan, star stuck, two meals away from turning West Los Angeles into a fire zone.

Now, walking toward the hospital towers, she finds this idea reassuring. Last night, after they tucked Ariel into bed, Max stood with her in the cool drizzle in the backyard. He said nothing could happen to her while they were together.

"I'll never leave you," Max said. "And I never break a promise." Then the rain stopped. Moonlight was falling on their bodies. She could study them as if they were in a photograph, leaded, a daguerreotype, perhaps. They were objects to be framed in metal and viewed by candlelight.

She reached for his hand and pressed it. There have been irrefutable vows and rituals between them. Their marriage is a kind of amulet. He is like a thin gold crescent or an antique crucifix she wears invisibly embedded in her flesh. There are numerous tribes where people die when they are hexed. If you are convinced a certain sequence of syllables can kill you like poison, then they will. Is that any stranger than casually strolling in front of a five-ton truck because a green light has flashed? she asks herself as she crosses the last boulevard before the hospital.

Yesterday it rained hard and Ariel was home from school. More celebrations for dead presidents with increasingly unsavory personal lives. The month has become a minefield for days off, and the laboratories and doctor's offices were closed. It was an extra day of waiting.

She took Ariel to the museum. A line had formed at the front door. A young woman with a red peony-print umbrella behind her said, "I've got to get something from my car. Save my place. I'll be coming back."

Julia stared at her. "I'm not on salary from this institution," she said. "I don't get paid for watching lines, monitoring behavior or giving instructions. It's not my fucking responsibility."

"How could you say that?" Ariel asked later. "I was completely shocked. You were so rude."

This is how we come to know the history of our state, Julia thought. We memorize what we are responsible for and what we are not. These are our rivers and mountain ranges, the borders, the way we know where we are. This is how we master navigation.

"I've got a lot on my mind," she told her daughter. "And anonymous line inspection is not on my agenda."

"Is something bothering you?" Ariel studied her face.

"Why do you ask?" Julia wants to know. She believes in fluid revelations, in connections that accrue through water. The child came out of her body.

"You always take me to museums when you have a problem," Ariel said.

Julia has spent much of her life preparing for the worst. She has premonitions of sudden lethal diseases. She experiences intense physical symptoms and frequent insomnia. She imagines earthquakes, car crashes, and the onset of virulent madness. She knows there is a type of arthritis that strikes in forty-eight hours and leaves the victim completely crippled, unable to bend enough to feed himself or use a toilet.

Now, standing near the museum in the rain, Julia realizes her fear of death has intensified since Ariel was born. She is constantly wondering how much of an impression she can make on her daughter before she dies. How much can Ariel learn from her, from Max? Will there be enough time?

Julia calms herself by recognizing that everyone can buy a year or two with chemotherapy. By then Ariel will be twelve or thirteen. She can play "Für Elise" now. She will play the *Moonlight Sonata* and Chopin waltzes by then. She will have read *The Diary of Anne Frank*. She will know algebra, how to read poetry and take photographs. She will know how to bake cheesecake. She will be able to do this completely by herself, including removing the pie tin with potholders. And Ariel will remember her.

It will be the same with Max, buying time. She imagines he will outlive the high end of the statistical predictions. And Julia tries to understand what a father can teach his daughter in eighteen months to prepare her for showing up at work, selecting a mate, raising children.

We live moon-to-moon, she thinks, entering the medical building lobby. This is why we are fascinated with pearls. How they are born in the mouths or bellies of oysters, how they are harvested and strung to the neck. These are a tangible reflection of the moons we live between. This is why they are precious and cost so much. They contain ideas of danger and power and outwitting borders, smuggling and time travel, how they are pieces of the same enormous puzzle.

Julia suddenly recalls a landlady she once had, Mrs. Jacobs. It was while Max was going to law school. It was a three-year period when she and Max were both drunk day and night. Later, she drove by the apartment and saw they had been living at the marina. There was ocean on the other side of their garage. She had been shocked to see this.

It was another rainy day when she was showing Ariel all the houses and apartments in Los Angeles where she had ever lived. Julia parked in front of the apartment and stared at the ocean, stunned. In the years they had lived there, neither she nor Max had ever realized they were across a driveway from the Pacific. They had thought the marina was a purely symbolic name, something with a Spanish touch. They could have seen sails simply by crossing an alley, but they never thought to look.

It was before Ariel was born. She used to hear the constant rattle of wind in tin or wind in metal. She assumed they lived near a reggae band that was diligently practicing. Or perhaps it was the site of a forbidden nocturnal festival, *santería* perhaps, where small birds were ritually slaughtered. And only years later, holding Ariel's hand, did she realize the sound was actually boats rocking against their moorings.

We are always rocking against our moorings, she thinks, visualizing Mrs. Jacobs. She seemed old to her then, forty-two, the age her husband is now. Mrs. Jacobs had a malignant tumor in her stomach. They were folding clothes in the laundry room. Julia asked her what she was going to do.

"Get a good haircut," her landlady said.

Mrs. Jacobs got a hundred-dollar haircut and a copper tint. She hired a photographer to take pictures of her naked. Julia told that to Max, one hundred dollars for a haircut and they had both been outraged by such extravagance. Mrs. Jacobs said she wanted proof of all that beautiful hair—for after chemotherapy. "I've always been proud of my hair," Mrs. Jacobs said.

Julia is standing near the elevator when she thinks she sees Martin, her first husband, the painter. It is a Martin as he would be now, heavier and grayer. Her perceptions have adjusted him the way computers transform photographs of children into the adults they will become. Many stolen children are found in this fashion. But Martin is dead. He had a heart attack in his studio last summer.

Julia often thinks she sees dead people, becomes startled and excited, raises a hand in greeting before she remembers. Last week she thought she saw her father, twice. Once he was driving a red pickup truck. Then she thought she saw her mother. It was a tall woman getting out of a Mercedes. A woman with a straw hat and a long suede coat walking quickly in the confused and lost way Julia remembers, the bold and somehow blind walk. Her myopic mother reaching out to a world that always hurt her. And she shouted, "Mother, Mother," and shocked herself.

Yesterday in the park behind the museum she was walking with Ariel in the rain. They were holding hands on a path smelling of citrus and eucalyptus. Ariel looked at her and said, "Mommy, don't do it."

"Do what?" She stared at her daughter. Ariel was wearing blue jeans with deliberate holes in the knees and thighs, and one of Knitter's psychedelic ponchos, which she has recently discovered and loves. She was wearing a paisley scarf around her neck and a navy-blue beret with tiny yellow daisies embroidered on it.

"Don't bury your spirit in another tree," Ariel said, not looking at her. She was holding her hand out and catching raindrops.

"You remember that?" Julia asked. It had been five years ago. She wasn't sure she had made an impression, had managed to engrave this into some fiber within her daughter. She was trying to impart not a memory, but something more subtle and raw. Julia is not immune to intimations about the future. In this she and Max differ. Max believes that the here-and-now and the yesterday are more than enough.

"Of course I remember," Ariel said. There was something sharp in her glance. "How could I ever forget?"

It had been a winter when she felt her mortality, relentlessly, monstrously. She wept when she saw suffering on human faces at bus stops and street corners, in elevators and supermarket lines. It collected around her, a private and unendurable gulf the color of smoke and lies.

One morning she packed a canvas bag and drove north with Ariel. Whenever Julia is overwhelmed, she thinks of Berkeley, where she spent the '60s, where she went to college, where she tried to stop a war and met Max. Berkeley remains a stable point, the breakwater when everything starts shaking.

She wanted to impart this to Ariel, to impress directly into her some primitive and irrefutable knowledge about place. Julia now recognizes she wanted to teach her daughter sorcery. They spent days walking through the campus, attending random lectures, riding to the top of the campanile, wandering through the museum and the boutiques on Telegraph Avenue.

Finally, sensing her daughter's restlessness, she told Ariel they would do something monumental that would last forever. Then she improvised a ceremony by a redwood tree. They spent the morning finding it, selecting it. Seven redwood trees from the bridge by the path along the creek leading to the Life Sciences Building. Julia had embraced the tree, breathed in an aroma of bark and sun on rot. There were tiny particles in the air like swarms of dissolving stars.

She leaned her forehead against the tree. Her head was burning. There was a forest within her and she could feel separate branches in flame. There are natural disasters one never hears about. We are defoliated on a lunch break and it doesn't make the evening news.

"My spirit is going directly in," she had informed Ariel. "Here. Feel." She placed her daughter's hand on the bark. "Now if you ever want me, if you need me and can't find me, my spirit is here."

Ariel had shrugged. Julia imagined she was dead, and an undergraduate Ariel, with her anthropology textbooks, leaned against the tree. Or an older Ariel, in transition or chaos, with an infant, perhaps, flying from Honolulu or Boston, renting a car, driving across the bridge, walking through the campus from Sather Gate, crossing Strawberry Creek to find her, and it must come from south to north, she is certain she explained this to her daughter.

"You left your spirit in Malibu, too," Ariel reminds her. They are holding hands by the eucalyptus trees behind the museum. "Remember? The pine tree on the cliff where the deer family had been sleeping? And don't forget the blue spruce in the park in Aspen."

Julia considered this information. Rain was falling on Knitter's coiled poncho. He died from a booby trap. He only lost one leg. He didn't have to bleed to death, but there was trouble getting the medics. Perhaps there had been a storm. Ariel doesn't know any of this.

"You're carrying so much excess baggage," a therapist she saw only once had told her. He was employing the expensive sifting-of-tea-leaves voice that she holds with utmost contempt.

"Baggage?" Julia had repeated. She stood up. "Like I'm dragging bundles of old clothes? I'm carrying artifacts that breathe fire. I'm talking about a language of smoke. These are three-dimensional creatures that can mate. I'd no more leave them go by the side of the trail than I would my child. I'll carry them until somebody amputates my arms."

Julia remembers this and smiles. She has decided to sit on a bench in a sort of impromptu plaza where she can watch both doors of the medical towers. She is waiting for her husband to return from the doctor's office where, statistically speaking, there is probably nothing wrong.

We live on a grid of numbers, on a kind of graph, she thinks. And soon she will stand in her kitchen and decide which pasta she will cook for dinner. A bus passes with an advertisement for the Bahamas and she considers the implications of green water lapping against intoxicated sand. She tries to remember what she has to pick up at the cleaners. It is the season of the tiger lily. Soon there will be the rising of snapdragons. She can sense their tentative powdery-yellow heads forcing their way from the dirt.

Max is walking through the glass doors into the brick courtyard near her bench. Julia is afraid to look at his face. We are always searching for a code to decipher the cycles, the peculiarities of personal geography, climate and circumstance, she is thinking. In a split second, he will see her.

Julia is sitting as all women sit after rain, when they have been redeemed and purified, draped in the silvers and pearl and pewter from an antiquity that cannot be lost. It is always an afternoon of secret and faulty resurrections. We are living moon-to-moon, searching for amulets on the edge of the fire zone, in a state of perpetual transitory grace. We are there on the banks of the great green river, with its derelict current and incoherent names, holding the hands of our daughters who will never forget where we have put our spirit or why.

our lady of the 43 sorrows

After the episode and what it did to the neurons in her mother's brain, a twisting and erasure so complex no one would ever be able to name or chart it, Tricia O'Shea was not the same. After the actual car crash Tricia O'Shea experienced a swelling in her skull so violent and extreme that the doctors were surprised when she did not die. It was a miracle, everyone said.

So this is a miracle in the age of the flexible spin, Cassidy O'Shea came to think. She thought miracles were horrifying. To see the cripple toss away his cane and suddenly walk was simultaneously startling and monstrous. And the blind man with his cataracts dissolved, with his vision suddenly intact. What if he were to look at the harbor for the first time and say, I imagined it would be bluer?

Cassidy walked on the bluffs above Santa Monica. The bay seemed stale and too placid. The water looked overmedicated. It was a Prozac harbor, manageable and contained, artificially tranquil.

It was the end of a cool summer and she had finally stopped making tangible plans for the funeral. She was no longer discussing hors d'oeuvres with caterers. This was the beginning of a new era. It was the period of the long return, not back precisely—Tricia would probably never be as she had been—but rather a return to some other condition where everyone involved could say they had done all they could. It wasn't about resurrection or restoration. It was about being thorough. It was about taking and retaking batteries of tests and making sure no one anywhere along the line could be sued.

Her mother was simply a faint mute pulse along the well-worn trail of the hospital corridors, the elevator to x-ray, the MRI room, the speech therapist, the overly optimistic driving coach. The insurance would not pay for such thoroughness. It took Cassidy an entire autumn to comprehend that. The insurance wouldn't cover her mother's walking or talking or driving lessons. It wouldn't pay for the instructor to try to teach Tricia how to move her fingers appropriately enough to dial a phone, to press a buzzer to let paramedics into her building, or to open a can. No one was talking about sonatinas. The piano was the first object Cassidy sold.

She thought her mother needed a counselor for her emotional problems. Of course, no one could suggest a line of treatment since her mother was now mute and her interior completely mysterious. Such a rehabilitation was considered experimental. Besides, Tricia went over the limit of her policy on the morning she came out of her second coma. When she was wheeled from the intensive-care unit later that week, she was already out-of-pocket.

Cassidy can remember the long return only if she establishes external increments. The standard demarcations have become useless. But she knows she sold the piano in winter. Then she found a dealer for the obviously good antiques. He took them piece by piece. By spring, even the rugs and lamps were gone.

Cassidy O'Shea realized this entire crash-and-burn drama was a scenario that she knew intimately. There were variations, but essentially it was about complete betrayal and absolute divestiture. It was about losing everything in slow motion even though you were a good girl and had done everything right. This was her personal Dust Bowl. She had been breathing it all her life, a vaguely metallic trace element that made her think of spoiled fruit and a knife in the back.

This was the season she discovered designer bullets. Cassidy O'Shea had always suspected they were there, in the too-warm afternoon air, in the drained aqua blue just behind her left shoulder. These were bullets that did not simply have her initials on them, but her full name, engraved. If they were ordinary bullets, a woman would have a chance. But these were designer bullets. They knew which way you would dodge, lean, zag, drop, and spin before you did.

It was ironic that this would occur during the year she was forty-three. It was when she had finally stopped saying she was thirty-seven. Women in their thirties looked different. Even she could see that. It was in the angle of the mouth, which seemed younger to her, virginal, as if there were words that had not yet been spoken. This year she recognized she was partway to fifty. This was the year of manifest tragedy. It was a sequence of losses so abrupt and enormous, so unexpected and indelible, that she kept waiting to collapse.

It was the year they wrote her further out of the script. First the leading man divorced her, taking a younger, thinner, blonder woman as his new wife. Then her popular son was given a spin-off marriage. And what was to become of her, Delilah Noire, the notorious tyrant? Once, Delilah Noire had been voted the most hated soap opera mother on daytime television for eight consecutive years. Now they had written her into perpetual intoxication. She only wore nightgowns and lurched into rooms to pour from a decanter and stagger to a sofa where she immediately passed out. She hadn't had a coherent line in three seasons.

Cassidy O'Shea looked out at Santa Monica Harbor as if the waves might produce from their coma of pale blue some sudden and unexpected revelation. She was seeking an explanation for the condition of her life. She felt there was some way in which her childhood in the Projects lingered legibly on her body. It was there, despite the university and drama school, aerobics and psychotherapy and voluntary community service, the theater projects for inner-city high-school students. There was a visible quality in her features, in the slope of her shoulders, perhaps, or in the back corridor of her eyes, that people could decipher. They sensed they could get away with it. They could leave her on the apartment steps to count cars passing on a boulevard, to spend four or five hours an afternoon doing that. It was a winter of rain. She was in first grade and her mother's new husband said she had lost her key and she couldn't have another. He would teach her responsibility. She was a bad girl. He knew that.

He recognized he could say that in front of her mother. He had perceived this just as the new producer did, that violation was possible, that there could be incursions across borders. The new producer sensed he could exile her from her husband and son and write her into an alcoholic stupor. He was certain he could get away with removing her ball gowns and cocktail-party dresses and replacing them with a rack of bathrobes.

There was a startlement and paralysis in her face that let her lover, Harry, know finally that when she delivered her flawless ultimatum, he didn't really have to divorce his wife and marry her like he had promised. He could just leave her on the corner of Doheny and Wilshire where she had leapt from his car, screaming. They had been lovers for six years and he finally realized that she could simply be deposited, howling and pulling out her hair, on a Saturday night street corner in Beverly Hills. He could simply drive home, and he did.

Cassidy studies the bay where there are no answers. Whenever she visits her mother, she parks on the cliffs above Santa Monica and walks slowly across the crumbling bluffs. On her weekly visit to Tricia's apartment she studies her series of disappointments, holds them from new angles, considers facets. It's a sort of review, an appropriate examination while walking on cliffs that are shedding. This is a season when Cassidy O'Shea is fully aware of the unstable nature of the ground she walks.

Today, in the haze of early morning near the ocean, she feels again that there is an indisputable way in which the Projects are still smeared across her face. It coats her body. That's why she spent her college summers working in a boutique in Boston learning color, fabric, line. She memorized how certain women who have never been locked out of their apartments walk. They take for granted there will be something they want. It will be unbuttoned and rebuttoned for them. There are rules, orders, methods that are accepted as reliable. Cassidy remembered how they looked at her without making eye contact. There was an art to that and to how they chatted and left with their purchases and would not have been able to pick her out of a lineup five minutes later. She studied their arms, how they carried their purses, their coats, their bags with tennis rackets. She practiced their accents, their walk. She learned more in the boutique than she did at the university.

Now, walking above the muted harbor, the apathetic and vapid suggestion of harbor on this morning without delineation, Cassidy thinks there is still an absence that festers, a gap where she could fall. Of course, there is the matter of money and debt. There is the possibility of a worsening. It is not the end of her forty-third year yet.

She shouldn't have been surprised by her mother's finances. There was something too distant and arcane to her mother's purported wealth. It was like a lie recited too often, too easily, each syllable locked into place. When Tricia spoke about the money she had put away for her, Cassidy trembled. Her mother was furtive. Cassidy didn't believe her mother was capable of leaving her an inheritance. It was probable that the properties and objects Tricia alluded to were fantasies. It seemed only a matter of time before her mother lost it all, whatever there was, entirely. It was Tricia's only psychologically viable alternative. In this respect, the car crash was a blessing.

Cassidy has come to know the full extent of her mother's holdings. She found out when she began to sell Tricia's jewelry. That had been the first clarification. Cassidy began with the centerpiece, the engagement ring from Tricia's first husband, Jeffrey Hamilton. Eight thousand dollars. Cassidy stood in the jewelry store after the appraisal. They had to bring her a chair to sit down in. Someone handed her a glass of room-temperature tap water. "You had expected more," the owner was sympathetic.

"Yes," Cassidy had responded, "much more."

But she was talking about her whole life, she knew that. It wasn't just the ring, which was merely symbolic, the dimensional residue of personal legend. The fact that Jeffrey Hamilton had given this ring to her mother while they were sophomores in high school, that her mother had to lose her virginity on the shore of a fetid lake so trivial it didn't even show on the map of the state, did not make the ring particularly valuable. Time had done nothing for the cut of the diamonds or their setting.

We live between these pathetic aggrandizements, Cassidy thought. It is only when confronted by debt and appraisal certificates that we are willing to admit this. Tricia's engagement ring had assumed the proportion of myth, a rite of passage beneath cottonwoods and willows on a night of irrevocable decision. In the end, such a juncture of blood and moonlight was worth eight thousand dollars.

That afternoon in the jewelry store she remembered when Tricia had told her she didn't need to study so hard. Graduating with honors wasn't required. After all, her mother had resources now. They were a long way from the Projects. Her mother said she didn't even need to get a degree. She had made good contacts. She could network now. That's what really mattered.

Instead of relaxing, or spending a weekend skiing, Cassidy studied harder. She went to the library immediately after the phone call from her mother. She felt spurred on, like she could run for miles, fast as a thick orange light. She felt like she had been shooting speed.

There was an overly ripe quality to all her mother's assurances. It was like a Los Angeles sunset where the colors aren't tropical but have the grain and sheen of metal. There was something too thin and gleaming in her mother's voice, as if she inhabited a private altitude where it was hard to breathe. When Tricia said, "I have sixteen river acres in your name. I have a horse ranch in Montana. Joey left me a piece of Palm Springs. I've got a block with fifty-eight rental units in Van Nuys," Cassidy wondered if she was lying.

It is her year of the lie, Cassidy decides. She is approaching the apartment where her mother now lives with Juanita, a young woman she has hired to be there twenty-four hours a day as cook, nurse, and companion. Juanita allows Tricia to wander through shopping malls and supermarkets. Sometimes they spend the entire day in the Beverly Center shopping mall. They can pass an afternoon in the pet shop. Cassidy has seen this, Juanita with the infinite patience for parakeets and cats and rabbits in cages. She allows Tricia to hold bunnies. They pet the FOR SALE kittens together. They scratch the backs of puppies. They stare at goldfish and angelfish in small tanks with plastic divers.

Tricia never took Cassidy to pet stores. She sees herself as she was at ten or eleven, standing in an alley waiting for her mother to come home. It is a California late afternoon. She is watching it become an evening and a night. A Santa Ana wind is blowing. Sunset smells of dust and tainted oranges, petals singed and fallen and baked into cement. It smells of blood on old bandages in locked back rooms where people are slowly strangling.

The wind is entering directly into her skin. She is without proper insulation. The climate is wrong. Her mother sent her to school without enough lunch money. She didn't remind her to take a sweater. The world is wire fences and flat streets with ugly fruit trees that birds have pecked off sections of. She is cold and hungry and she doesn't have a watch or a key.

Cassidy believes it possible that this internal geography is somehow physically manifest. It is this configuration that is somehow apparent. Her producer and the writers can decode it in the texture of her skin. She has purged it from the fabric of her aesthetics, her opinions and politics, but the residue remains on her body. Harry, her lover, saw it.

It is the year of the lie. Now there is the situation with her mother and the properties. The so-called river house on sixteen acres in upstate New York was a derelict cabin in a forest gutted by loggers. It looked ripped and scarred, as if someone had made an X on a map and sent mercenaries out to enact it three-dimensionally. The land was actually worth less now than when one of Tricia's husbands had bought it. There had been talk of a resort then, a renaissance that wasn't even a pulse anyone remembered.

This was Cassidy's one scouting expedition. She considered going into Boston, taking the train perhaps, to see if the boutique where she had learned how to become a woman was still there. She decided against it. After this, she was satisfied to simply talk to real estate agents long distance. The ranch in Montana proved to be merely barbed-wire fence around mountains with nothing but trees on them, one hundred sixteen miles from a town. On closer inspection the house in Hawaii was actually owned by a syndicate of which her mother had less than a tenth-share. This was how it went, delving into what Tricia had proudly called her portfolio, how she had made it sound like a sort of treasure chest.

Now, standing near her mother's apartment with the cliffs of Santa Monica Bay behind her, it occurs to Cassidy this is precisely what she had intuited all along: the fantasy stock and property portfolio, along with the safe deposit box of marginal jewelry, two squash blossoms and a fetish necklace a man in a shop on Melrose told her she wouldn't be able to give away. Cassidy has at last and finally opened the cupboard and it is bare, exactly as she knew it would be.

Cassidy glances at the ocean, at what might be the ocean but what is now the identical shade as the sky and air, a vague veiled gray haze that makes her think of asthma. She is standing above the harbor at Wilshire Boulevard where there is a statue of a woman. Cassidy assumes it is Saint Monica and she has never before felt so close to idolatry. Cassidy could herself be bronze-coated. She could be rooted in the poor soil above the abstract Pacific. They could call her Our Lady of the 43 Sorrows. She has one for at least each of her years.

What does it matter? The bass and halibut have already left the harbor. There is nothing safe to eat in these waters. Perhaps it is time for a new guardian, a new witness. Maybe she could audition. The role wouldn't be substantially less than the current incarnation of Delilah Noire. At least she could stop pouring cold tea into a plastic goblet. She could stand on the bluffs rather than curled drunk on a sofa. It would be more challenging.

It occurs to her suddenly, walking the last hill toward the apartment she has rented for her mother, that Delilah Noire is as far as she is going to get. This is her division, a sort of light middleweight. She isn't going any higher. She isn't going to Broadway after all. She will continue pouring pretend whiskey and collapsing in her bathrobe until they decide they don't require her services anymore. Then she will do what several of her unmarried friends do. She will teach acting. There are voice-overs, commercials, trips to Asia and South America where she is still one of the dragon ladies of daytime television. She has a certain popularity in Taiwan. It is almost a cult. She could endorse products there. Also in Singapore and Argentina where they have named a perfume after her character. It smells like glittering mangoes, like fruit with ground-up razor blades and sequins in it. It smells like why children shouldn't go out trick-or-treating anymore. Still, they would pay all expenses. A hand cream here, a hairspray there. It could be made to add up.

And who knew what the future would bring? Cassidy turned around suddenly, glanced at the pale gray inkwell in the distance that is the statue of a woman she has decided must be named Saint Monica. She should be subtitled Our Lady of the Sorrows, watching the withering waters, witnessing the stained waves beneath the haze dragging themselves in and out. This season I am Our Lady of the 43 Sorrows, Cassidy thinks. But who knows what the next catch will bring in?

Her mother and Juanita are watching Spanish television. They are eating buckets of take-out fried chicken. Her mother has an apple pie with a soup spoon jammed into it balanced on her lap. There are pizza boxes on the floor. There are no napkins. Juanita and her mother are watching cartoons that have a garish sound track. They are laughing.

Even Juanita looks heavier than she remembered. Her mother has gained more than seventy-five pounds since the car crash. None of her doctors mention this.

Cassidy O'Shea talked to her mother for half an hour, employing a variety of intonations and physical gestures. Tricia did not move her eyes from the television screen, not even briefly, not once. Cassidy handed Juanita an envelope of cash and walked out.

Later that afternoon Cassidy had her secretary arrange a cruise to China for her. The show would be on hiatus for two months. Cassidy felt that the China Sea was in order, Hawaii to Taiwan, Hong Kong then Thailand. Perhaps six weeks of salt water could be a sort of cure. Who could predict how the market would be when she got back? Maybe Tricia's silver mines would have suddenly come in. Perhaps the writers would take the bandages off old Delilah, the reliable war-horse she had become, and let her speak again. In any event, it was time to absorb a chaos of blue that had nothing to do with dust and oranges and standing hunched in the shadow of hibiscus hedges on the side of an alley in West Los Angeles waiting for her mother to come home. It was time for a sky that didn't look strung with metal, clouds erased, and in the soiled air a sense of sutures and wires. Besides, Cassidy reminded herself, it is always sound practice to take a cruise between disasters.

When she returned to Los Angeles eleven pounds thinner, sculpted by thousands of miles of cobalt-blue water seen alone, the producer said something about meeting with the writers. A recovery program, perhaps. They were kicking that around. Delilah Noire going into detox and rehab. Maybe she could do an AA thing. Public confession followed by a spiritual conversion. There were outlines on paper. Conferences were being scheduled. There was enthusiasm.

She drove to Santa Monica to tell Tricia. Of course, she never knew what Tricia did or did not hear. No one could even offer a speculation. Her brain was irreparably damaged in an entirely unique way. The doctors said they could write up her mother's case for future study. They kept saying that, but no one bothered.

It is a day when haze has settled over the bay and the air, water, and sky are the color of a void. Vacancy is not empty. It is filled with something like Santa Monica in the morning. It is not ocean but the suggestion of ocean. It is the implication of sand beneath light fog. There is the sound of water, indistinguishable from the traffic on the Pacific Coast Highway. It is all a sort of subsound, metallic, like what you imagine you hear on the periphery when you're half asleep on an airplane. It is not a sound, precisely, but a taste that is tinny and sharp and awful. It makes you think your mouth is bleeding.

Cassidy O'Shea knows that this journey to Santa

Monica is not about telling anything to her mother, who can't hear words, probably, or even organize sound. She imagines her mother's head is a kind of aviary or carnival, corridors of bells and bird calls, calliopes and tambourines. The circus is always in town. Or maybe Tricia can hear the breathing of stars or the passage of electricity in wires that must be a yellow brilliance like horns. In the darkness, perhaps her mother listens to a chorus of small flames.

Cassidy recognizes that her pain is largely symbolic. It's an ancient wound and suddenly she can define it. It's about ineluctable destiny. It's the central core we can't disguise or run away from. The designer bullets know our secret heat and they can seek us out in any climate, no matter how much therapy, dance, and yoga classes we have taken, no matter how we have forced ourselves to develop discipline and values. It doesn't matter how well we have brought to bear intelligence and will on personal history. There is something ticking that we carry. It is these circumstances—these intricate private geographies we bring with us the same way we carry diseased cells or abnormal chromosomes—that give us cystic fibrosis or muscular dystrophy.

It has been eight weeks since she had seen her mother. Tricia has no sense of time. Cassidy remembers taking Tricia for a final tour of the house in Brentwood before the new owners moved in. The furniture was gone, the personal effects, but she thought her mother might be jolted into recalling something.

They sat in the garden together. Her mother was holding a box of chocolate candy. She wasn't looking at the pink and yellow rosebushes, the purple iris, the slant of sun across the beds of white lilies she had planted herself. She held a chocolate between her fingers. "I love—" Tricia took a deep breath, "—candy." Then her mother put the chocolate in her mouth. It was the first time she had spoken since the accident.

There had been a moment in midsentence when

Cassidy thought her mother would speak her name. I love, her mother said, and the world stalled, as if it were a vessel that had dropped anchor. It would come now, finally. And Cassidy would forgive everything. It would be the moment of the one hundred thousand perfect white lilies, an entire mesa of calla lilies in wind. The afternoon would deposit them like a form of rain. They would fall from the clouds, a faint white scent like the memory of bath powder. The benediction would be late, but it would still be on time. Then she watched her mother close her mouth around the candy and look away.

Cassidy paid off certain debts with the profits from her mother's house. Then she hired Juanita and rented Tricia the small apartment near the ocean. She deliberately chose this setting because she entertained the notion, subliminally, that salt water could heal. Once her mother had a boyfriend who owned horses. They went to the racetrack at Del Mar in the summer. This boyfriend would take them to the beach in the early mornings and show them the horses being walked through the waves, the injured horses, sore legs dancing through blue salt. It was curing their wounds. Even though she realizes, rationally, that Tricia can't determine if she is in Pasadena, Pittsburgh, or Paris, Cassidy wants her near the water. She believes it is possible something can happen in Santa Monica, perhaps from the wind while her mother sleeps. Perhaps some aberration in the current.

It is before noon and her mother and Juanita have just wakened. There are bags of breads and pastries on top of the television. Juanita claims to be nineteen but Cassidy thinks she is younger. Juanita comes from Guatemala and she has a story Cassidy doesn't want to hear. She knows Juanita is alone in Los Angeles, she wears a crucifix around her neck, goes to mass on a regular basis, can read simple signs and has incomprehensible patience for a brain-damaged woman who is mute and does not understand her language.

Juanita does the cooking. Tricia cannot even be taught

to open the refrigerator. Her mother had awakened one day, as if from one level of evolution to another, and she was hungry. She ate uncontrollably. Popcorn and crackers, chocolate and cakes, foods she had never eaten before. Her mother, who had spent decades subsisting on mineral water, diet sodas, and salads now ate bags of chips dipped in butter, melted cheese, and barbecue sauces. Her mother weighed over two hundred pounds. The flesh on her upper arms hung like thick webs and seemed translucent, as if you could see the air as it passed through the room. Her arms were turning into appendages that might have an aerodynamic function.

Last spring when Cassidy noticed that her mother's ankles were bloated, she took her to a mall and bought her thongs in primary colors. She purchased dozens of extra-large muumuus with orchids and plumeria on them, with flowers her mother did not seem to recognize. Cassidy didn't expect her to. The woman who gardened and drove a white Cadillac and smelled of new leather and suede, of almond hand lotion and tea-rose soap is gone.

"I don't want her in the house all day," Cassidy had instructed Juanita when she was explaining the appliances, locks, and alarms. "Take her out when the weather is good," she pantomimed. Someone on the set had written this for her in Spanish and she recited it. "The salt air is good," she hoped she was saying in Spanish. She repeated it twice.

Juanita seemed to agree. She dressed Tricia in an orange and pink muumuu of what might be enormous peonies. She carried a shawl for her and an umbrella, just in case. Then they would get on the bus in front of the apartment and ride downtown to Grand Central Market where Juanita occasionally met a third cousin for lunch. Sometimes she walked Tricia around Chinatown or Olvera Street where Juanita bought her churros and doughnuts when Tricia pointed and stamped her foot. There were dancers with long red ruffled dresses and castanets in the plaza on Olvera Street, and strolling mariachis near the shops. Then they took the late afternoon bus back to the ocean.

Cassidy considered her mother, hurtling through a city of her own device, watching it unfold from the window seat of a bus. Her mother up high, the city miniature like a child's building block set at her feet. Tricia, bouncing up and down in her bus seat, a first grader again, perhaps, in a land of perpetual field trips. Tricia quivering with excitement, the purple-and-yellow plumeria of her muumuu violently shaking. Her mother, a hurricane above an island she doesn't remember. There are no failed marriages, abandonments, or lies, no daughters left to spend afternoons on the side of alleys. There is nothing to confess. She is erased, the marrow of pure. And it occurred to Cassidy O'Shea that her mother was the happiest woman she knew.

As Cassidy prepares to enter the apartment, to sit amongst the bags of fudge and cupcakes, she is paralyzed by an image of her mother so startling that she often sees it in precise detail when she closes her eyes. She envisioned this as she stood on the deck of the cruise ship on the high seas going to China. The sea was a cobalt-blue film, mottled like marble, like the face of a drowned woman, in which she saw a single scene relentlessly repeated.

It is always exactly the same. Her mother is walking toward the bus with Juanita. Her mother is holding Juanita's hand and laughing. Cassidy has accidentally encountered them on the street. It is summer and she had been walking toward them for several blocks but only at the last moment recognized them. Her mother, vast, a ruined garden, lumbering and smelling of rancid butter and cooking oil. She had run up to her, had wrapped her arms around her and pressed her face into her mother's flower-print breast, into the grit of salt across her bosom. The scent of garlic and chili was rising out of her pores. Her mother had looked directly at her and said,

"I love—" and in the pause Cassidy closed her eyes, "—Juanita."

Then they were getting on the bus. Her mother had a window seat. She was holding an enormous bag of popcorn in one hand and a box of a dozen jelly doughnuts in the other. Tricia was staring out the window, not at her, not at Cassidy who is ridiculously waving, not at a strip of accidental yellow canna near the bus bench, but at something else entirely.

For one partial instant, for one fluctuation of the soul, Cassidy thought she was searching for her ten-year-old daughter, the one she left alone after school without a watch or a key. The daughter she seemed to have misplaced when she was working, between marriages. The little girl standing beside a broad boulevard littered with occasional palm trees. It is a late afternoon washed by a corrupt magenta sunset, pitted by a desert wind filled with sand and obscene suggestion. The child with the cut knee and stomachache, the one who wants a kitten, who collects pictures of cats from magazines and doesn't get to go to the pet shop on the weekend, is waiting for her mother to come home. And as Cassidy O'Shea watched the bus turn the corner, she finally knew, absolutely, that her mother was never coming back.

Kate Kiernan

about the author

Award-winning author **Kate Braverman** is a cult writer who has been publishing poetry and experimental fiction since 1972. Raised in Los Angeles and educated at Berkeley, Braverman expertly weaves her California experiences throughout her work. She was a founding member of the Los Angeles Women's Building and the Venice Poetry Workshop. She has written four books of poetry, three novels, and two short story collections. Two of her books of poetry were nominated for Pulitzer Prizes, and among her published stories are an O. Henry Award winner and several that were selected for the Best American Short Stories 100 Distinguished List. Braverman lives with her family in the northern Allegheny mountain region of New York.